Fractured

Heart

A SMALL TOWN ROMANCE NOVELLA

ESME LENNON

Tainted Town

Book cover by Artscandare

Edited by Ria at Moon and Bloom Editing

ISBN: 9781666407747

First edition 2024

Please note:

The Tainted Town series and The Sin City series are intended to be a story-with-plot within a shorter book. These novellas are fast-paced and don't have as much depth as a full length novel. This is because my novella series are written with the purpose of giving slower readers a story line to follow, plot, and spice, but with a short page count. Please keep this in mind while reading.

Trigger warnings

This book is intended for adult readers only, due to the content included.

Trigger warnings:

Domestic violence/abusive relationship, emotional abuse, explicit sex scenes, 8 year age gap, murder, violence, talk of drugs and alcohol, cheating, gaslighting, use of a gun, use of power, blood, cigarette burns, description of injury, pregnancy.

For those who keep their emotions locked inside their heart.

It's okay to let them out.

You're human, after all, and that makes you stronger than you know.

Playlist

1. Red Hot Chili Peppers – Death of a Martian

2. Wolf Alice – Feeling Myself

3. Sarah Cothran – Stronger Than Me

4. Digital Daggers – Surrender

5. Fleurie & Tommee Profitt – Breathe

6. ADONA – Haunted

7. Red Hot Chili Peppers – Under the Bridge

8. The Neighbourhood – Reflections

9. Teddy Swims – Lose Control

10. Ellie Goulding – Like A Saviour

11. The Weeknd – Where You Belong

12. ADONA & Seibold – Crazy

"When the whole world is silent, even one voice becomes powerful." – Malala Yousafzai

Contents

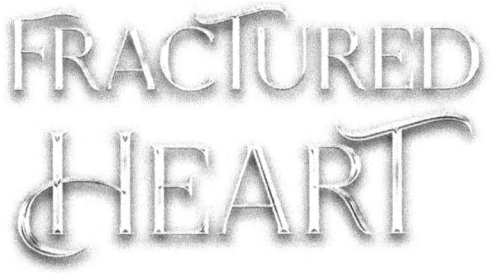

She doesn't need a saviour...
She needs to be set free.

1

ELLE

"The grace of the Lord Jesus Christ be with you." The words leave my lips as the rest of the church repeats the usual phrase back to the priest. A humid day in Charlestown has me fanning myself with a leaflet of upcoming church events, trying to dry the constant sweat beads gathering on my forehead.

I try to focus on what the priest is saying, but my ears zone in on anything and everything else that's happening in Charlestown Church. A dry cough from the back row, a young child playing with his toy car, someone gulping water. Anything to distract myself from my husband's hand on my thigh.

His touch controls me, keeping me in place and behaving like the young, innocent wife he so desperately wants me to be. And he gets what he wants, because he knows I'd never step out of line. A well respected councilor in this town comes with responsibilities and we always have to maintain our appearance of being a loving, happily married couple. Even if it's a complete and utter lie.

Directing us to our feet, the priest starts singing a hymn, using his hands to encourage us to sing along. Out of tune and someone in the back row singing the wrong words, the full church hall pushes their passion forward and makes the priest proud. I'm not sure he'd be so proud if he heard Charlestown's members singing without the belting organ in the background, but what he doesn't know won't hurt him.

I watch the clock as it strikes a minute closer until the service is over. Ten minutes, five minutes, then one. Moving painfully slowly, but moving nevertheless. I wasn't brought up religious, and that hasn't changed since turning twenty-four. Attending church is simply for my husband and our community. Gossip in Charlestown is like a sport, and I certainly don't want to give the older ladies any ammo.

A few more readings and a couple more hymns brings the service to a close, and as much as I'd love to go home to my golden retriever, Poe, it's a Sunday tradition in Charlestown to head over to the beach for the markets. By beach, I mean pebbled sand which hurts your bare feet and a simple sea front, with no piers or beach huts. It's not popular for its attraction, more its location. A strip of Charlestown's most popular stores and restaurants sit along the seafront, bringing in all the locals and visitors.

Stanley's arm snakes around my back, guiding me out the church and across the road. Looking like a caring husband, he checks the road is safe before we cross, but I know it's not for my safety. A councilor showing up at Sunday markets without his wife is not a good look.

It doesn't take Stanley long to engage in business chit chat, giving me a chance to slip away and browse the markets. Small business owners set their products out on collapsible tables under gazebos, ready and prepared for church to finish. They rely on Sunday markets to make the majority of their wages, so I'm always eager to purchase and support the locals. There's everything, from fruit and vegetables, jewelry, meat, local groups and books. There's something for everyone, but my eyes narrow in on the flowers.

It's like floral heaven here, with so many different kinds of flowers that I need a picture book to spot which flower is which. Tulips, roses, lilies, peonies; my eyes beam at the glorious dream in front of me. While most people have family, friends and a partner in their life to bring them happiness, I don't have the privilege of that. Instead, I get my happiness from Poe and flowers. Flowers take me back to my childhood, waltzing through the flower store my mother worked at. It was brightness and bliss and a happy youth. A feeling I'm sure I'll never feel again.

"The purple gerbera daisies please." I smile at the florist while pointing towards my favorite flower. The sea crashes in the background as the waves kiss the sand, the tide making its way out into the depths of the ocean.

"Good choice." The voice is so low, it gains my attention immediately. Mandarin and leather invades my nostrils before I even allow myself to glance.

Passing the florist a twenty-dollar bill, I turn my attention to my left to offer a quick glance, but I'm taken aback by the man gazing back at me for a response. Around six feet tall, nearly a whole foot taller than me, brown eyes, a sleeve of tattoos on his left arm, short stubble, and golden brown hair. I have never seen him here before.

I snap my attention back to the florist in hopes she'll engage in conversation with me, but she's too focused on arranging my daisies in the most perfect way. My body is telling me to glance around to find where Stanley is, just so he doesn't see me talking to this man, but I'd look more suspicious searching for him. So I do the only thing I can in this awkward moment.

"Are you new here?" I ask, keeping my eyes on the flowers before me. I catch myself twiddling with the stems and leaves on the table, in hopes of making myself look busy and distracted.

"Yeah." I feel his gaze on me. "Moved into the new place on Aspen Avenue." He clears his throat. I know the place. It's not often Charlestown has new, fancy housing built here, but that's not the only reason I know the exact place he's talking about. My good friend Pria once gave me a tour of the exact apartment, thanks to her new boyfriend, Tristan, and his estate company selling the property.

"What brought you to Charlestown?" Curious, I ask, wondering why anyone would bother with this small town when places like Casamount City exist.

"Work."

This time, I can't stop my eyes from shooting his way. "Work?" I question, my brows raised in shock. It's not like Charlestown has a bunch of amazing job opportunities.

He nods. "Yeah, work." He must note my surprise, because his eyes squint as the corners of his lips tilt upwards. "Do people not work here?" His tone is playful, but I don't entertain it.

"Well, yeah. It's just, Charlestown, out of all the places in the world?" I can't stop my brows from frowning.

"I like small towns," he states plainly, turning his body towards me. "This one seemed perfect."

"Hmm." I nod, unable to agree with him but not wanting to scare him away. Just because Charlestown isn't my dream location, doesn't mean it can't be his.

The florist has my flowers perfectly bunched and hands them over to me with a beaming smile on her face, which I return. My nose automatically lands on top of the daisies, inhaling their pollen scent, and I find myself heady as it reaches my lungs.

"Violet?" My eyes shoot to my left, confused by what this man is talking about, so much so that my words don't bother forming a response. I just stare at him like I don't speak the same language.

His finger shoots up and points at me, repeating the same word, but this time I follow his finger and catch sight of my purple collarbone tattoo. It takes me a second to figure out that he's pointing at what he thinks is a violet.

Amateur.

"It's a daisy." I correct him, somewhat offended he thinks it's a violet.

"Why is it purple? I thought daisies were white?" I can't tell if he's fucking with me or if he's genuinely being serious. Judging by his dipped eyebrows, I think he's actually being serious.

I don't waste my breath explaining, instead, I point to the purple daisies in my hand and give a 'there's your answer' smile.

He nods, and it looks like he's about to say something, but a voice I know all too well interrupts us. "Good choice, love." Stanley glances at my flowers and puts an arm around my shoulder, pulling me into his side. I feel my muscles stiffen, but I force them to relax. We're in public. It's appearances that matter.

"I don't believe we've met, I'm Stanley Adams, Town Councilor." Stanley holds out his hand with his usual winning smile plastered on his face.

"Johnny." He shakes his hand in return.

So, he has a name.

"Are you new to town?" Stanley presses, keeping his fake friendly persona but trying to do what he does best, pushing for information.

"Yes, sir. I'm here for work." Johnny nods, his shoulders back and his stance bold. He's taller than Stanley, but he seems kinder. Gentler.

"Charlestown? For work?" Stanley's tone is curious; he doesn't miss a chance to find out what he wants to know.

"That's exactly what-" Johnny holds his hand up towards me, "I don't believe I got your name?" He questions, and I feel Stanley's grip tighten on my shoulder.

I gulp and prepare to answer, but Stanley beats me to it, taking control of the situation, as always. "This is Elle, my wife."

I don't miss Johnny's split second of shock when he hears 'wife'. He recovers almost instantly, so quickly that Stanley didn't indicate he noticed.

"Nice to meet you, Elle." He holds out his hand, to which I pause, but Stanley pushes me forward an inch, so I return the shake. His hands are warm and firm, but tender. Like he can hold the weight of the world but he wouldn't dare do harm.

"Likewise." I nod, pulling my grip from his and resting it on my side almost instantly.

"That's exactly what Elle said." I almost get whiplash from everything that happened in the past ten seconds, but my brain adjusts and remembers the conversation just before our introductions. "I take it most people don't move to Charlestown to work?" Johnny inquires, but he already knows the answer from our previous conversation.

"Not often." Stanley chuckles, but it's like his mind has suddenly switched. He pulls Johnny into a hug and mutters something to him that I can't quite hear. I'm curious and my brain is telling me I need to know, but before I can take any action, Stanley turns to me and tells me he's introducing Johnny to some friends.

Nodding, I watch them waltz away, thankful I made it out of that interaction unscathed. No sly comments and no whispers from Stanley.

Inhaling and exhaling a deep, warm air, breath, I calm my senses and walk over towards the other stalls, taking in all the items and relishing in my own company.

2

JOHNNY

This town is like a goddamn cult.

I spent most of yesterday people watching from a distance, paying close attention to a few people in particular. Those being the town council and the police force. That was who I was supposed to be watching, and I did ninety-percent of the time, but it was meant to be one-hundred-percent. I didn't think my attention could ever be yanked away from my targets, but a five-foot-two blondie has proved that wrong.

And I'm pissed about it.

My jaw clenches. I'm thirty-two years old, I shouldn't have infatuations.

I'm fucking good at my job, that's why I was sent to Charlestown to investigate. I'm a highly recommended private investigator that has a one-hundred-percent success rate. So, when my focus is diminished by anyone I'm not supposed to be watching, sirens are immediately raised in my mind.

I'm here for a job, and that's what I intend to do.

Rule number one about going undercover is to blend in. And what's more blended than becoming the mayor's security? He'll always be the focus of attention, no one will look past him, which is where I'll be. Invisible in the background. Close, but not seen.

Close enough to get intel and overhear conversations that aren't for public consumption, but trusted enough to never repeat or relay them.

A mistake, if any.

Fastening my tie in my bathroom mirror, I adjust my cufflinks before making my way into the kitchen. The open plan style apartment means my living room and kitchen are spacious and well lit, with no stairs or walls blocking my route. The matte black decor creates a calm vibe, giving me the perfect place to work and relax.

Grabbing my listening device off the kitchen counter, I attach a microphone inside my breast pocket and connect it to my phone to collect any evidence. Immune to metal detectors, I can get inside the mayor's office without raising any warning signs.

Grabbing my wallet and my keys, I make my way out my apartment and to my car. A short drive into the center of town and I'm at my new job location. I park in staff parking before making my way inside.

I'm ten minutes early, but practicality and time-keeping will build a positive character view of me. Often, positivity leads to trust, and I *need* their trust. Trust breeds secrets and secrets are the downfall of many.

I count on that downfall to ultimately ruin this town and make it a better place. To get rid of the toxic people and have them face their punishment.

"Johnny Miller!" My attention snaps to the doorway to my right, my posture straight and a light smile on my face. "Mayor Clyde, it's a pleasure to meet you." A hand is placed in front of me, and I grasp and shake firmly. His salt and pepper hair is receding and his large build gives him a slight limp. Wrinkles frame his face and the dark circles under his eyes show how tired he is.

"Pleasure is all mine, sir." I nod before adjusting my suit, making sure there's no interference on the device.

Following the mayor's lead, he welcomes me into his office and points at the oak colored chair, opposite the desk. I take a seat as instructed, before setting my eyes on the room layout. A rectangle shaped room, with an oak and burgundy color theme and matching paintings throughout. One wall covered by filing cabinets and the opposite wall has a full length bookcase with numerous golfing trophies and books that are gathering dust. The far wall has a large, arch window that is no doubt one way glass, with us having a clear view of Charlestown's busy roads. The burgundy textured wallpaper around the room looks like it was pasted over textured walls, with small rips and uneven bumps beneath.

Sliding a phone and an earpiece across the table, Mayor Clyde lifts his hand, encouraging me to insert the earpiece. "This is your work phone. Any emergencies will automatically be transferred through the earpiece. You'll attend all work duty visits with me for protection, and for your own safety, we'll provide you with a bullet proof vest and a gun."

My eyebrows shoot upwards. "Do you get people shooting at you often?" I question, a hint of playfulness to my tone.

Clyde shrugs and scrunches his nose. "Not once." He pauses. "But never say never, right?"

Clyde's chuckle fills the room, and I join in. Even though it's not remotely funny at all. My throat itches from the forced laughter. One point to me for bonding with this asshole.

A loud ringtone interrupts our laughter, and I have to bite my tongue to stop a smile from growing on my face after watching Clyde struggle to get his phone out of his pocket. His grunts and twists to maneuver the phone from the pocket is ten times harder than it needs to be. Turns out he's a lazy bastard that doesn't want to stand up to make a job easier for himself.

I take his distraction as an opportunity to pick out disguised spots to plant hidden cameras or microphones. The dusty books are looking like a good spot. I notice some smaller trophies on a lower shelf which are less loved than the golfing ones. Discreetly leaning on my right arm to get a closer look, I notice the plaque writing on the trophies. It doesn't take a genius to realize they're his kids' trophies. Both male and female soccer trophies, displayed not so proudly, and collecting dust like the books.

It seems Clyde's accomplishments are more important than his childrens, which doesn't come as a surprise to me. It seems like the kind of selfishness he'd present, but it doesn't stop my heart from clenching at the thought of his children assuming their father proudly presents their trophies at work, when that's not the case.

The phone call ends abruptly and Clyde's grating voice pulls me back to reality. "The wife," he begins, "wants me to take the kids to soccer practice but I'm playing a few holes with my buddies at the club." He sighs and frowns, like his wife is the one in the wrong here.

Every cell in my body is telling him to stop being a bastard and give his kids the attention they deserve from their father, but I force that temptation away. Instead, I just nod, not entertaining him further.

"You married?" Clyde's sudden question catches me off guard, but I don't show it.

"No, sir." I shake my head, curious as to where this is going. I'm trained to not give out personal information, but if there's one button I can press here, it's to give off a lonely persona. If Clyde feels bad for me, he'll welcome me in.

"Girlfriend? Kids?" Clyde presses.

"Nope. None." I shrug, relaxing back in my seat.

Clyde bobs his head, but doesn't say anything. His silence lets me know the gears are turning in his head. He doesn't know it, but I've just planted a seed in his mind. One that'll encourage him to view me as a confidant.

A few raps of a knuckle against the door and a female's voice speaks seconds after. "Sir, the sheriff is here to see you."

"Thank you, Kandi." Clyde nods, but rises to his feet before Kandi can even leave the room. "Johnny, come meet the sheriff. He works very closely with the mayor's office to keep everything running safely and smoothly."

Yeah, I bet he does.

I rise to my feet and adjust my suit before following behind Mayor Clyde. We take a short walk down the corridor and pause outside a no entry door. I assume we are waiting for the sheriff, but Mayor Clyde takes a quick glance up and down the corridor before swiftly entering the no entry door.

Entering a room that looks like a cleaning storage closet, the sheriff stands in the center of the room, smoking a cigarette. The smoke is thick and gray, the vile smell attacking my nostrils and threatening to make me cough. The blinds are closed and the room is dimly lit by saver lights, casting a shadow figure of the sheriff.

"Johnny, meet my brother, Sheriff Peter Beasley." Guiding his hand towards the broad figure, I see a hand reach outwards in greeting. "Pete, meet my new security guard, Johnny Miller."

Brother.

I don't waste any time gripping Sheriff Beasley's hand, even if it is sweaty and calloused. "Pleasure to meet you, Sheriff." Nodding, I quickly back up, desperate to get away from his deathly cloud of smoke.

He nods his greeting and engages in a conversation with Mayor Clyde. It's almost like I'm no longer in the room as they both face each other, crack jokes and talk about how many holes they're scoring later. I only hope they're referring to golf.

Connections are firing in my mind as I note the family connection. Not only are they both men in a work position of power, but they're brothers. Two people who love and trust each other.

I was warned about how tight-knit the town officials are here, but a family connection is next level. It's not a case of only worrying about their own safety. It's a case of two brothers. Brothers who will die for each other, fight for each other, and defend each other. Hardwired to protect each other.

That's usually a quality I appreciate in a person. But not when they're the suspects in a drug trafficking investigation.

An investigation I'm undercover for.

3

ELLE

I count the seconds before Stanley leaves the house. Each tick sounding loudly on the grandfather clock, echoing throughout our home. An early breakfast each day ready made for Stanley before work, we sit and eat the croissants and fresh fruit I prepared together. Eight o'clock, I head to the dressing room, put on one of a hundred summer dresses I own and get myself ready for the day. Eight thirty springs around, and I kiss Stanley goodbye for his day at work.

Yet my favorite sound is when the door clicks behind him and he's out the house. Watching him take step after step, further away from me, before hopping in his blue Camaro and speeding off.

Tension dissipates from my shoulder and I allow myself the first deep breath of the day. This house is exquisite; a two-storey brick exterior, with white pillars, a black door, and large windows. White and caramel brown interior, with bright features and old wooden furniture. It's the perfect picket house, yet I never feel at home here.

It's not my safe space. Anywhere with Stanley isn't a safe space. I feel like I'm constantly playing the game operation, petrified to make the slightest mistake, knowing it'll cause him to get spiteful.

But I'm stuck with him for life and I have to accept that. Or until I can at least afford to escape.

Heading into the dressing room, I pass the white rails of clothing and my white dressing table, until I kneel in front of the vent. Twisting the two secure pins, I pull them out and yank the vent free, revealing my study books.

I grab the books, my laptop and my pencil case and search for a bag to put them into. My emerald Chanel bag catches my eye first, but I search for something else. Bundles of clothes are shoved along the rails as I rake my eyes through the gaps, but I'm hit with defeat.

The Chanel bag it is.

I don't enjoy parading Stanley's money around, nor do I like the gifts he gets me. It's for appearances, and a councilor's wife can't look cheap. If it was up to me, I'd have a ten dollar tote from the market, but Stanley thinks they're 'cheap trash, not worth a dime'. Money really is everything to him.

Fixing the vent back into place, I shove my books in my bag and rush downstairs. I grab Poe's lead from the hook by the front door, I fasten him in and we dash outdoors, locking it behind me.

My red Audi sits in the drive, but I don't bother to drive it. It's been sitting there for months, undriven, waiting to get at least one use out of it. But I have no desire to drive it. In fact, walking around Charlestown is my favorite thing to do. I feel free, alive and uncaged. The fresh air kissing my skin, the sun warming my body and light chatter filling my surroundings, I imagine a life where I'm in control. One where I can wake up in the morning and lay in bed for an hour. One where my cheeks hurt from smiling too much. And one where a constant state of anxiety isn't my norm.

One day.

The twenty minute walk into town center is enough to give me a clear mind and to tire Poe out so I can study with no distractions. Located on the edge of the town center is a small cafe, so small that you wouldn't know it was there if you weren't already a regular. Other than the small 'Cosmos Cafe' sign in the window, it looks like a small home. Luckily for me, it's never busy and I've never seen a familiar face there, so I don't have to worry about being spotted.

The entry bell rings as we enter and my eyes instantly fall on the green plants hanging from the ceiling. Square wooden tables, cushioned seats, and a fuschia orange theme throughout, the small space creates a homely and comforting vibe.

We take our usual seat in the back corner, Poe curling up under the table as I pull my laptop from my bag. Automatically connecting to the WiFi, I load up everything I need before heading to the counter to get a coffee.

I'm met with a woman with short auburn curly hair, black frame glasses and bright red lipstick as she wipes down the sides, singing along to *I Only Have Eyes for You* by The Flamingos.

"Hey, doll!" Her greeting is pure, a beaming smile instantly lifting her cheeks. "Same as always?"

"Yes please, Angie." I respond. A smile tugs at my lips as she gets to work.

Quickly spinning on my feet, I grab my wallet and pull out the cash I have stashed in there. Any spare change I can get my hands on from Stanley's account without ringing alarm bells finds a place in my wallet. I can't have Cosmos Cafe showing on our bank transactions. Having no access to my own bank account and only being allowed to use Stanley's means he can track my every move, and if he found out I was studying, he'd lose his shit. That's not a risk, it's a deathwish.

I place the change on the counter and slide it over towards Angie's side, watching her work her magic.

"I'll bring it over to you, doll." She calls over her shoulder, not even giving me a chance to protest.

Nodding, I turn on my heel and take a seat back at the table. My eyes flick over the tasks I need to complete today on my laptop screen before I grab my headphones and place them over my head. *Death of a Martian* by Red Hot Chili Peppers flows through my ears, silencing the outside world and turning my focus up to one-hundred.

I flick through this year's curriculum, mentally weighing up and planning everything I need to do. When I need to come to the cafe and when deadlines are due. It's my final year of studying after a two-year break and it's the only thing in my life that I give one-hundred and ten percent. It's my lifeline, literally.

My brain flashes back to three years ago, my first year of college at Pineridge University, strolling campus without a care in the world. Life was so easy back then; attending classes as an undergrad student, getting my teaching degree and taking a creative writing class on the side, just because I loved the idea of letting my brain run free and expelling any thoughts I had on my mind, down on paper. It gave me a kind of freedom to get my emotions out in a controlled way.

And then I remember my third year of college, trying to maneuver intense studies while grieving the death of my mother. My walls were caving in and I felt suffocated by my own emotions. I felt as though I'd lost a piece of myself. The part that gave me joy and happiness. The part that wanted me to live life to the fullest. That part of me is now buried with my mother.

Pria always reassured me it would get better, that life is full of tests and we can either give it our best shot and complete it, or let the waves of challenges weigh us down. I wanted to believe I could choose the first option, but since then, my life has been a constant freefall. Just as I think things can't get worse, I get smacked in the face with another complication that turns my life on its axis.

And instead of venting my emotions, I have no choice other than to keep them locked inside my chest. The only person I feel safe venting to is Pria, and I still can't bring myself to tell her the real reason I'm married to Stanley. It'll be knocking down a line of dominos; every single lie lined up after telling the first would come to light and my life would be ruined.

Poor Pria thinks I'm with Stanley because I actually love him, because he treats me right and our thirty year age gap isn't an issue because we fell head over heels for each other. I scoff at the burning lie. I can't even tell Pria that Stanley is a councilor because they're severely disliked in Charlestown due to their constant bad decisions. I lied and told her he's a cop, which isn't much better, but it saved me from getting attacked with judgy eyes.

The real reason I'm married to an asshole like Stanley is a secret I'm never willing to repeat, nor explain. My shame wouldn't let me sink that low, only to gain sympathy looks and apologies for my own mistakes.

Angie places my coffee down in the center of the table, careful not to knock any of my study books, and places a plate with two muffins in front of me.

Confused, I catch her eyes. "What are these for?" I question, the fresh chocolate scent filling my nostrils and making my stomach grumble.

"Study aid." She winks, before turning to walk away.

"Let me pay for them, please." I plead, loud enough so she can hear me as she walks away.

"Not a chance." Angie calls over her shoulder before chuckling to herself.

My heart swells from Angie's constant hospitality and care she sends my way. She always looks after me, letting me use the cafe for hours at a time and always giving me free food. She doesn't pry into my situation, instead she just lets me do my thing and doesn't bother me.

My fingers find my keyboard and begin tapping away, writing word after word for my essay due in a couple weeks. My eyes pick out important sections of information from my study books, before typing them down. I find the perfect groove as time slips away and I get sucked into a study bubble. Poe snoozes away under the table and gets regular treats from Angie as she passes by, keeping him content just as much as me.

Angie passes me by slower than her usual pace, but I don't look up to see why. She must be cleaning the counter or fiddling with the display pastries. I see Poe's tail wag from the corner of my eye under the table, and my heart blooms to know he has someone like Angie to trust.

But the new scent in the room has me freezing on the spot, my fingers hovering above the keyboard as my eyes widen. Mandarin and leather fills the small cafe with its strong scent, and in that exact second, my body runs ice cold from realization.

My head isn't even given a chance to lift itself to investigate before Johnny takes a seat in the chair opposite me. He places his coffee on the placemat in front of him and leans back in his seat, his muscled arms placed on the arm rests and his legs spread.

His brown eyes stare at me like I'm a television show he's interested in, making me feel like I'm under interrogation. I swallow back my nerves and take a deep breath. He can't see my laptop screen and there's no one other than Angie around, so no prying eyes can see us.

Pushing my headphones back to fall around my neck, I pull my laptop screen closed and straighten my shoulders. "Aren't you supposed to be working?" I challenge Johnny's gaze, hoping he would take my unsociableness as a sign to leave me alone.

"It's my day off." He states plainly, his eyes taking in the scenery of the cafe.

"Hm." I nod. "Didn't realize security had days off."

Johnny scoffs as the corners of his mouth tilt upwards. "And how would you know what my job is?" He pries, resting his elbows on the table and leaning forward. His frame is wide and intimidating, but I try to ignore it.

"My husband is a councilor. You work for the mayor. It's a small town, word travels fast." I confirm, sipping my third coffee refill.

He nods, but doesn't say anything. He just sits there, staring around the cafe before staring at me with that annoying smirk on his face. I wait him out, desperate for him to leave so I can focus on my studies but not bold enough to ask him to leave.

"Why aren't you working?" He finally cuts the silence with a knife, but doesn't even give me the chance to respond before his eyes squint at the table.

I follow his eyes, curious to see what he's confused about, but curiosity is replaced with overpowering trepidation. He's looking at my study books. Not looking, reading my study books.

My body moves on its own accord as flight mode kicks into action, grabbing my books and shoving them into my bag so he can no longer see them. Panic washes over me as I mentally dig inside my brain for a solution, anything, to get me out of this situation.

The weight inside my chest from my heart sinking physically hurts as I acknowledge the connections here; Johnny and Stanley work in the same building and will cross paths. If Johnny mentions he saw me here, let alone studying, my life will be a disaster.

Johnny watches me, but he doesn't say anything. Instead, he has this look in his eye, like he's more concerned about me than what was on the table. I don't read into it. Instead, I pack my things away into my bag and unplug my laptop charger like urgency is of the moment.

"Hey Violet." His voice is soft but I don't respond. My hands begin to shake as my heart pounds like a hammer in my chest at the thought of him knowing someone else in here, another person who could link this to my husband. But as I lift my head, there's no one else in the cafe.

It takes me a second to realize he's talking to me. Yet, he got my name wrong. Recollection springs to the front of my mind, reminding me of the flower stall in the market, and his mistake of calling my tattoo a violet instead of a daisy.

"I need to go." My throat is like sandpaper and my words are barely audible, but he hears me anyway.

"Hey, it's okay. Just breathe for a sec." He rises to his feet and grasps my forearms, the gesture gentle but it feels like it's scalding me. "What's wrong?"

I have a second of vulnerability. The longest second of my life spent convincing myself I can confide in him. That he could help or at least comfort me and tell me everything will be okay. Then reality takes over and reminds me Johnny is a stranger. Someone who's an outsider and someone I could never trust. He's the person who could ruin me by telling my husband what he saw me doing at the cafe.

I shake my head as my mouth opens and closes. "Please," I croak, unsure of what I'm asking him for. "Please don't tell anyone."

Johnny recoils as he tries to figure out what should be kept a secret. "Tell anyone what?" He questions, his face scrunching up like it's a tricky request.

"That you saw me here." I circle my finger around, implying the cafe. "And that you saw me studying." I grab Poe's lead and sling my bag over my shoulder before Johnny has time to think of a response. "Please." A final plead for him to keep this between us.

The door is the only thing I have my sight on as I make a beeline for the exit, not allowing my legs to stop until I'm far away from here. Picking up my pace, I speed walk and then jog along my route home, sending glances behind my shoulder to check Johnny isn't following me.

I don't stop until I'm inside my front door, finally allowing myself a gasp of breath. My thighs ache from the constant movement home and my heart feels like it's about to pound out of my chest. It's now I allow myself to let the fear and anxiety building up from the cafe exchange to exit my body.

Sliding my back down the cool wooden door, I curl up into a ball on the floor and allow my tears to create paths down my cheeks.

I'm trusting a man I don't know to keep a promise.

Something tells me this isn't going to end well for me.

4

JOHNNY

First time visiting Cosmos Cafe and I'm leaving with mental whiplash.

I came across the cafe by chance and thought I should learn about the town a little more. I was expecting it to be small, considering it doesn't even look big enough to live in, but I was pleasantly surprised to see it almost empty, bar the owner and the blonde mystery herself, Elle Adams.

From what I thought could be a simple interaction, her sudden worry strikes me as unsettling. Nothing she was doing was out of the ordinary for a normal person, so why was she frantically worrying I would expose her?

Inserting the key into my front door, I swing the heavy wood open and shut it behind me. Slinging my keys onto the table, I grab my laptop and stroll over to my breakfast bar.

Taking a seat on the black stool, I open my laptop and switch it on, loading up the intelligence database. The crime agency I work for has done some basic recon on our targets, so I have some intel to look over. My eyes gaze outside my second level window, taking in my perfect view of the back of Charlestown Church. My eyes catch on a few passerbyers, carrying groceries and walking their dogs.

This town is seemingly innocent at first glance. It's a typical small town community filled with friendliness and respect. But once you find a small crack in the surface, there's a whole new world below, full of corruption and debauchery. I'm yet to figure out if the people of Charlestown are aware of the scum that runs their town or if they're clueless. If there's one thing I know about corrupt town officials, it's how well they cover their back. They're different people inside. They've mastered the act of putting on a friendly, welcoming face, just to hide the fact they're a vice to this town.

I bring up the evidence files we have on the council and the police department, scanning important information and broadening my search to their family members. The best way to get information is to befriend and become a shoulder to lean on. It only takes a slip of the tongue for their wife or child to mention a passing comment, giving me a whole new world of intel and a new lead to follow.

I browse Sheriff Beasley's file, flicking through his family and noting local places they visit. Overhearing conversations is a blessing; most people mind their own business in public, but I do the opposite. I listen to every single word, zeroing in on hushed conversations and observing the sly looks over their shoulder. If they think no one is listening, they'll sing like a canary.

I make a mental note to visit their frequented areas.

I do the same with Mayor Clyde and his family, noting their regular patterns and places they visit often, adding them to my list of places to visit.

The pulling in my chest is telling me to go off course and branch out my search, but I ignore it. There are still multiple connections and leads within the police department and council that I need to explore.

But it doesn't go away.

It tries to grab control and encourages me into giving in.

Straightening my legs, I don't let my temptations get the better of me. I head over to the coffee machine behind me and begin making myself a black coffee. The liquid trickles into my mug as steam rises, wafting the strong scent of coffee around the air.

My foot taps and my fingers fidget on the kitchen counter as I try to ignore the deafening devil on my shoulder, enticing me to give in. The angel is no fucking help, sitting silently and forgetting to remind me to focus on the issue at hand.

The coffee takes longer than Marvel credits, mocking me by being slower than usual. It's like it's baiting me to give in to my selfish demands.

Fuck it.

I take three steps back to my laptop and trail the cursor over to the search bar. With a few clicks on the keyboard, I type in Elle Adams and click search. Research photos collected from our private investigation agency pop up; a handful of shots of Elle, all with Stanley, completing daily errands, leaving church and at the market.

There are only two photos of Elle by herself, leaving and entering Cosmos Cafe. I'm curious to know why she only goes to the cafe alone, considering every other outing, she's glued to Stanley like he's her lifeline. I know she's not cheating on him because she was there alone, and if she were cheating, why would she go to a cafe instead of somewhere private, like the safety of her own home?

Alarm bells sound in my ears at the unease filling my body. Something about Elle and Stanley's marriage is off. Other than the fact he looks like he's edging towards a retirement home and she's young enough to be his daughter.

Scrolling down on Elle's file, I find their marriage certificate.

Married three years ago. She was twenty-one and he was fifty-one.

Elle was away at Pineridge University a month before their marriage for three years. Nothing on her file about studying currently, though.

I try digging further to find out how and when they met, but her file is recent, leaving me with nothing but unanswered questions.

I want to know everything.

No. I *need* to know everything.

Why she's with a man who spends most of his time trafficking drugs rather than paying attention to her. What makes him so special that he's worthy of her time. What does he have that made her vow to be his wife?

Fuck. Why is she so goddamn intriguing?

Loud ringing jolts me back to reality, pulling my attention from my laptop to my phone. I check the caller ID, swipe the phone to answer and place it on loud speaker.

"Scout." I say as a greeting, my attention half on my best friend and half studying the photos of Elle.

"Damn, Johnny. You sound happy to hear my voice." Scout teases, sounding somewhat breathless on the other end. "Is work intense?"

"Intense is a word for it." I respond. "This town is," I sigh, rubbing my palm down my face, "it's something."

"Everything good?" Scout questions as concern laces his voice.

"Yeah, man." I reassure him. "You'll be here soon enough. When do you transfer fire stations?"

Scout grunts on the other end of the phone, probably doing one of his many fitness workouts. He claims it's because fire-fighters need to stay in shape, but I don't think they require him to work out twenty-four-seven, which Scout pretty much does.

"In a month or two. Is there anything I need to know about Charlestown before I make the move?" I can tell his tone is joking, so I don't bore him with the things wrong with this town.

"Attend Sunday markets. They're big on it here."

Scout scoffs before I give him a basic rundown of stores and things to do in Charlestown. Reassuring him I'll keep an eye out for available apartments nearby, he gives me some of the firehouse gossip.

I try to focus on the words coming from Scout's mouth as he waffles on about firehouse gossip, but my attention is focused on zooming in on a photo of Elle's daisy tattoo.

Supposedly a daisy.

Definitely a violet.

5

ELLE

It's been a week since I saw Johnny at Cosmos Cafe and it doesn't seem like Stanley has been informed about my secret study sessions.

I'm thankful for that, but dread also sinks deep into my stomach knowing Johnny is holding onto something that can ruin me. My brain tells me he's going to use it against me to get what he wants, like a twisted puppet master.

Exactly like Stanley did.

I prepare the fresh duck, roasted potatoes and grilled asparagus ready for when Stanley returns home from work. The table is laid out ready with cutlery and wine glasses and I decant a bottle of pinot noir and place it in the center.

Preparing dinner is a routine I could do with my eyes shut. Stanley expects to be fed as soon as he's home with his favorite wine at the ready. The flame burns orange on cream colored pillar candles in the center of the table, the smell of magnolia filling the air.

Gazing down my apron to check my outfit looks okay, I center myself and check the time. The grandfather clock dings at six o'clock, like a warning siren, letting me know Stanley will be home any second now.

Twenty seconds after six and Stanley strolls in the door, his shirt messy and his briefcase slumped next to the front door. He loosens his tie and chucks it on top of his briefcase, his shoes placed next to the shoe rack.

Weighted footsteps sound louder as Stanley makes his way into the kitchen, my body instantly stiffening at his front pressed against my back. My guard is instantly up the second Stanley is near, like a silly attempt to protect my feelings from whatever insult he's planning on throwing my way.

Like a child, he sits in his seat at the table and grasps his knife and fork in both hands, tapping them on the table, silently demanding his food. It takes him ten seconds before he begins asking how long dinner will be and I suddenly feel a sense of urgency to get his food in front of him.

Stanley is intimidating enough on a full stomach, I don't want to face hungry Stanley. I can just about bare two glasses of wine Stanley.

The oven timer dings and I grab the oven gloves to extract the food. The scent of a freshly cooked meal fills the air, steam lifting off the duck and potatoes. Oil bubbles at the bottom of the cooking tray as I place it on the side.

Giving Stanley more than double my portion, I dish up our food and place his plate in front of him. You'd think he's been starved for days by the way he shoves his fork into a scalding hot potato and shoves it inside his big mouth.

Like he already forgot the food just came out of the oven, he opens his mouth and breathes quickly before letting the potato fall back onto his plate. "Why didn't you tell me it was scorching hot?" He pours himself a glass of wine before gulping down the lot, then he pours himself another glass and pours a small amount into my glass. "Are you trying to punish me or something?"

Worry fills my features as I try to calm Stanley down, even though he brought this on himself. "I'm sorry." I apologize, standing to get him a glass of water. "I thought it would have cooled down a little by now." I place the glass in front of him and take my seat.

A scoff leaves his lips, but his shoulders are risen and filled with tension. "You could have checked it before me." He plays with his food before placing the exact same hot potato back in his mouth. "Is that why you haven't started eating yet?" A full mouth full of potato is laced with an accusatory tone.

I feel the familiar strain between us starting to build. Like a volcano, Stanley always starts off his verbal abuse with passing comments and a joking nature, but it doesn't take him long to bubble and erupt, spitting insults and indignities my way.

"What? No! I would never purposely hurt you." I defend myself, trying to keep my features soft, despite the anxious river beginning to take me under.

His gaze penetrates me, like he's zoning in on his target and he's ready to pounce. But then his gaze falls to his food and he starts playing around with his duck before shoving a slice into his mouth. Silence surrounds us, other than clattering cutlery against the porcelain plates.

I allow myself to release a breath to relax myself within the sudden stillness between us. One would think this is the end of our conversation, but I know better. Stanley is just getting started.

Stabbing my fork into my potato, I cut a small portion off and pop it into my mouth. I repeat this over and over again, just so Stanley can see I didn't do anything on purpose. My untouched glass of wine stares at me, waiting to be consumed. I've never been a big drinker, but since seeing how it changes Stanley, I steer clear of all alcohol. If a few glasses of wine can bring out his worst side, I'm afraid to see how it affects others and even myself. I want full control over myself and I can't do that when liquid is altering my mind.

"How long did you cook the duck for?" The quietness around us is shattered when Stanley opens his mouth, his tone sharp.

"About one hour and fifteen minutes, with ten minutes cooling time." I confirm, placing a slice in my mouth, even though nausea is beginning to build in my stomach.

A hum vibrates in Stanley's throat as he takes another bite. "It's overcooked." He states plainly, shaking his head.

My mouth opens to apologize but he doesn't give me a chance. "You know, Elle, I work hard so you can have a perfect house to live in. Your dog can have a home and you don't have to work." He pushes his chair backwards, a deafening screech penetrating the air. "And this is how you repay me?" His head tilts to the side slightly as his piercing blue eyes bore into mine.

I try to protest as I shake my head, ready to repeatedly apologize and take the numerous insults coming my way, but

Stanley is up on his feet. His mouth is pulled into a thin line and I tell myself anything that's about to leave his mouth isn't true, but he's stained me with so many insults in the past three years that I've started to believe them.

Grabbing his newly topped up glass of wine, he takes a gulp and places it back on the edge of the table. One hand on his hip and the other scratching his head, he takes short, loud breaths as his anger starts shadowing his face.

His usual shouting corner is within the back left of the kitchen, his eyes focusing on the familiar area. But before he can make his way over there, he steps on Poe's paw and Poe jolts, knocking into the table in the process.

It all happens in a flash.

Glass dotted around the floor with stains of red wine accompanying each delicate shard. I snap into a panic bubble, trying to figure out a way to diffuse the situation before it gets to a breaking point.

Before *I* get to my breaking point.

Shooing Poe out the room, I make sure he's behind a closed door so his paws don't end up sliced and bleeding. My ears ring from Stanley's raised voice, screaming everything I do wrong and how much of an awful wife I am.

But divorcing me would never cross his mind. He has his own puppet and control is something that man craves.

I begin placing the shards in my hand, not noticing the shake that's taken over me. My heart pounds in my chest as my stomach churns from the familiar dances that lead up to Stanley's breakdowns. I can't catch my breath, but I can't stop cleaning either. I need the problem to go away, so Stanley has a chance at calming down.

My legs feel like jelly as I try to stand up, my free hand grasping the table for stability. I take a few steps away from the table to deposit the glass into the bin and grab a towel to clean up the wine.

Crouching back down, I smear the beige colored towel over the spillage, soaking it up and removing the issue. "It's okay." I stupidly attempt to reassure Stanley. "It's all clean now." I ball the towel up and place it on the kitchen side, ready to go into the laundry.

"Okay?" Stanley growls. Pointing towards the door where Poe is safely secured, his face begins turning red and his brows dip with widened eyes. "That fucking dog!" His scream is laced with poison. "It's his fucking fault. He needs to be taught a goddamn lesson!"

Stanley's feet take him towards the door and I'm stuck in time. Seconds feel like hours and my brain is firing, trying to tell me the best thing to do.

My hands press onto Stanley's chest, stopping him from advancing onto Poe. I'd never forgive myself if anything happened to my boy. He's my refuge in this shattered world. "Please," I plead, tears brimming my eyes. "It was my fault."

Terror is all my body is running on right now and time has suddenly sped up. It's no longer letting me take time to think things through, instead it's chucking me in the deep end with no action plan. It's simply leaving me in a situation with no control, forcing me to navigate these events without a tour guide.

"Damn straight it's your fault!" I see fire burning in Stanley's eyes, close enough that I feel the heat radiating off of him. "He's your dog, control him!"

"I will." I attempt to reassure him, but the brimming tears falling from my cheeks seem to do nothing for Stanley.

"You're crying?" He mocks me, his tone belittling. His towering figure blooms over me like a night shadow, my body instantly recoiling from him. "You're goddamn crying when I'm the one who has to live with a rabid dog and an attention seeking wife!"

A loud ringing pierces my ear, my vision blurred. Searing pain assaults my cheek as throbs and aches begin growing. I can't focus; my mind is a tornado as I try to make sense of what just happened.

Stanley's red face turns a sudden shade of pale, his face suddenly wide eyed and open mouthed. His unusual startled expression flips my panic meter up to one hundred. My middle finger caresses the shooting pain on the side of my face, a hiss leaving my lips as soon as I touch the sore area. My finger is warm and damp, but it's not until I look down that I notice it's blood.

Blood from my cheek.

It feels like a weighted block is sitting on my chest as realization starts painting a clear path in front of me.

Stanley hit me.

He's never hit me before.

I can't think straight, my flight telling me to get the fuck out of this house but Stanley's apologies and display of love screams louder.

He says he's sorry. That he never meant to hurt me. He's had a bad day at work and life is just testing him lately.

He says lost his temper and he'll never do it again.

And despite his obvious excuses, I still choose to believe him.

I feel numb.

Every inch of my body is senseless, my mind dull from last night's dinner. The only place that feels something right now is my swollen, purple cheek, lined with a crimson cut. I brush my fingers over the raised skin, instantly wincing at the contact. Sharp pain zaps my cheek, forcing my fingers away. I suppose it's not that bad. It could have been worse.

The thought forces bile up my throat.

I want to erase last night from my memory and never be reminded of it ever again. Maybe if I tell myself nothing happened last night, I'll say it enough to actually believe it.

Stanley seems to have forgotten about it already. Like every other morning, he waited for his breakfast before getting ready for work and dashing out the door.

He didn't acknowledge my bruised face. His apology last night was enough to ease his conscience. I take that as a good sign though. Maybe that means the situation got out of hand and it was a one off blow in the moment. He said he wouldn't do it again.

I stare at my own reflection, my heart breaking at the girl looking back at me. Twenty-four years old and damaged. This is not how I pictured my future, but beggars can't be choosers, and that fits my own situation a little too well.

A loud bell jolts me from my thoughts, my eyes suddenly gaining focus and my ears following the noise. Grasping my phone, I check my texts.

Stanley: Left my planning permission folder at home. Bring it to the office ASAP.

Groaning, my eyes automatically roll at Stanley's demands.

Me: Sure.

Chucking on a short sleeve white, floral summer dress, I fix my hair and get Poe leaded up, ready for the stroll to the mayor's office. I glance at my cheek, moving my head from left to right to see if my hair covers the purple swelling.

It doesn't.

I rummage through my makeup drawer to find my concealer and powder, and try my absolute hardest to hide this monstrosity on my face. Multiple layers of thick liquid and repeated painful squinting later, I powder my cheek before double checking how well I did.

Not bad.

Grabbing the pumpkin colored folder from Stanley's office, we make our way out the door and head into Charlestown center.

The glowing sun and distant waves instantly lift my mood, reminding me that even though most aspects in my life are on a constant downfall, there are small pleasures that are within reach. I just have to step out from the darkness to touch the light.

The front entrance to the mayor's office is almost always occupied by visitors and employees, so I decide to take a more discreet route. Rounding the rear of the office, I spot the councilors entrance and head towards the door. It's not a door for public consumption, but considering my husband's position, I take the risk and hope for no consequences.

Pulling the cool steel door handle open, I quickly glance around behind me to check no one has spotted me, before making my way inside. The door is hidden down a thin corridor before branching off into the main building, so seeing many people here is unlikely.

I take a moment to readjust to my surroundings, trying to remember which way Stanley's office is when entering from the opposite direction, but as my feet take me forward, the hardness bumping into my chest stops me.

Stumbling backwards, Stanley's folder falls from my hands as I attempt to grip onto anything to steady me. Nothing but slippery walls laugh back at me as my hands slide downwards, but before I meet the floor with a hard thump, a large hand grips my upper arm, pulling me upright and steadying me.

"You good?" Low and curious, the question pulls my attention. My eyes are focused on the muscular chest in front of me, pecks chiseled so strong that the outline is prominent through the black t-shirt. His large arms are enough to make me gulp, my eyes instantly settling on the tattooed sleeve on his left arm. I know exactly who it is.

Johnny.

Meeting his oak eyes, I ignore his furrowed brows and worried expression. "I'm fine. My mistake." I wave him off, bending to pick up the fallen folder before attempting to slide past his stationary body. He allows me to pass and pull my shoulder in so I don't touch him, not releasing it until I'm past him.

"Wait." His tone is zipped, making me freeze on the spot as I face away from him. "Turn around."

I frown, my face scrunched at his sudden request. Slowly, I turn my body to the right until I'm facing him. "What?" I snap, my tone irritated.

His facial expression hasn't changed and he just stares at me with empty eyes. I start questioning whether he's belittling me, letting me know he still holds my secret in his hands, ready to drop whenever he pleases.

"What's that?" He grunts, his eyes still fixed on mine.

"What's what?" I respond, looking around the room for some kind of clue for what he's implying.

His calloused hand is suddenly on my cheek, tilting my head to the right. It takes me a second to realize what he's studying, and before he can get a good look, I smack his hand away.

My surroundings are suddenly quieter as my panicked heartbeat thumps in my ears, my stress levels suddenly increasing. My paranoia kicks in like a lightning bolt, side stepping Johnny to escape his pointed questions.

He mirrors me, stepping in front of my exit route and not letting me leave. "Elle." His tone is abrupt. "What happened to your-"

"My dog ran into me while he was playing fetch." I snap, cutting off his sentence. He's observant and somehow spotted my heavily concealed bruise, raising alarm bells in my mind. If he noticed the bruise, what else does he pick up about people? Me? The thought leaves me filled with unease that I need to escape this man right this second.

"Seriously?" He answers, not convinced.

Shit.

"Mm-hm." I nod. "He's clumsy." Johnny just stares at me, no emotion or movement on his face. It's intimidating, and if I don't get away from his towering presence soon, I'm scared he's going to unravel more about my personal life.

I see the small space under Johnny's arm and take the chance while I have it, dipping under his arm and speed walking to Stanley's office.

I get deja vu reminding me of the last time I ran away from Johnny and I try not to laugh at the chances of it happening twice. He's around every corner I turn and I'm sure he knows more than he lets on.

And I don't like the power that comes with knowing secrets that could ruin someone's life.

Mine specifically.

6

JOHNNY

I've been in my job long enough to know when someone's bullshitting me. And that's exactly what Elle did. While the bruise itself could have come from her dog, her reaction tells me that was a downright lie. People don't get defensive from honest mistakes. They get defensive when their lies are unraveling.

I don't like to speculate on what someone is going through in their personal life, but after years as a personal investigator, you learn to pick up signs and actions. Things that aren't normal reactions.

I want to press further, but she won't tell me anything when she feels like she's backed into a corner. I need to coax it out of her on her terms. Let her know that she can trust me.

Can she trust me?

I'm here to investigate her husband. If she found out, she wouldn't trust me with anything. Unless, she really needed someone in her corner. An outlet for her situation. And as much as I take my work seriously, she piques my interest in ways I've never experienced.

I want to know everything about her. How silky her delicate skin is. If her laugh sounds as angelic as I imagine. What she looks like when her mouth falls open and soft moans escape her plump lips when she comes.

My jaw clenches at my own unprofessionalism.

I'm standing in Charlestown Church at Sunday service and all I can do is think about Elle, about the thoughts and feelings she provoked when I saw her at the Mayor's office. If God is real, I'd be up in flames for the sins I'm committing.

I'm only attending church to keep an eye on my targets to see how they act. I've come fully equipped with a microphone attached to me because the council and police department often use the markets as a subtle meeting spot. It doesn't look suspicious and people know better than to interrupt men in power when they've in conversation.

Working at the Mayor's office hasn't given me much intel, yet. Most conversations are about women or golf. Things I have no interest in. I knew I'd be playing the long game here, though. They need to find out whether they can trust me first, and by earning their trust, I don't push them for anything more than work related information. I keep my head down and do my job. Being a fly on the wall is the best way for their information to slip out.

As soon as the service comes to a close, I make my way out the exit before people have even risen from their seats. Stride after large stride, I make my way over to the beach across the road and blend into the markets. My eyes fixate on the wooden church doors, giving each pedestrian exiting a quick once over. If they're no use to me, I move onto the next. Eventually, my targets of interest begin leaving. Sheriff Beasley, Mayor Clyde, a few councilors, police department deputies, and Councilor Stanley Adams. As expected, his arm is tightly gripped around Elle's waist, keeping her close enough that she may as well be glued to him. It's like she's his sick trophy; he parades her around like a proud owner, desperate to show off what's wrongfully his, but Elle is just there to keep her mouth closed and look good for his appearance.

Wearing a pastel pink short sleeve summer dress, her short blonde hair is barely touching her shoulders with two shorter pieces at the front. Pretty pink cheeks glow as the sun rays hit her, her skin sunkissed. But her features are dulled. Heavy eyes, no smile lines, straight eyebrows; she looks numb. The sight of her makes my chest tug. Does she even have something to live for?

My mind automatically picks out important character assets, things that would tell me significant information about a person. Shaking my head, I focus on who is of importance here. While Elle catches my attention unwillingly, I'm not here to watch her.

Even though I still do.

Her attention is glued to a handmade mug gazebo, and I watch her as her gaze flicks between Stanley and the gazebo. Stanley doesn't even give her a glance, his attention fully focused on Sheriff Beasley. Even Sheriff Beasley doesn't acknowledge Elle, even though she's his sister-in-law.

Squinting my eyes, I shake my head at their lack of interaction. How can they simply not notice her? She's a blooming flower in a wheat field, impossible to miss.

I lipread Elle asking Stanley if she can head over to the mug gazebo, yet he barely offers her a nod before turning back to Sheriff Beasley. He treats her like an unwanted child, yet remains married to her. So many unconnected ends with unanswered questions.

Elle's tense posture relaxes with each step away from Stanley and her aura perks up slightly when she reaches the mug gazebo. It's not until a golden retriever appears from behind the table that she smiles fully. The first actual smile I've seen on her face, and *damn*, it's as heavenly as I imagined. Risen cheeks and a warm and wide smile with perfect white teeth.

A fucking beauty.

I try my best to blend into the olive green gazebo backdrop as Elle strolls my way with her dog and a tennis ball. Peeking around the side to watch her, she waves the tennis ball side to side while her dog jumps up and down excitedly, hopping next to her as they walk away from the markets and down the beach slightly.

I watch as she throws the ball as far away as she can, waits for her dog to catch it and lets him drop it into her hands. Flicking my gaze to the left, I see Stanley in deep conversation with a few men dressed in checked trousers and a polo, and I know he's too interested in golf talk to notice anything his wife does.

My shoes sink slightly in the pebbled sand as I take each step closer to Elle, small crunches sounding below me. Waves crashing in the distance as the tide goes out to the unknown, a few fishing boats dotted far out in the ocean.

Within a few feet of Elle, she's hyper aware of someone within her personal space as her shoulders tense and her body movements almost slow to a stop. I don't like the idea of her fearing who's behind, so I announce myself.

"Who's this?" I question, crouching next to her standing body and stroking the ball of fluff, minimizing myself and allowing her to stand above me.

Her gaze immediately falls down to me, and I swear I see her shoulders relax a little. I can't see the bruised cheek, but she could have covered it up. I'm still not satisfied with her answer, but now isn't the right time to pry.

Her eyes flick to her dog before collecting the tennis ball. "This is Poe." She responds before throwing the ball. Poe shoots off like a firework, his eyes glued to the neon green ball.

"Star Wars fan?" I ask, rising to my full height. My eyes are focused on her, but I still keep Poe in my peripheral vision.

"Mmhm." Nodding, she doesn't spare me another look.

Elle's guard is still up and I notice her eyes flick to her left every few seconds. I know she's watching for Stanley, whether that's because she wants him over here or if she's seeing if he's watching us. I have a feeling it's the latter.

I don't want her to feel afraid, so I take a few steps away from her towards Poe. He drops the ball in front of me, so I bend to pick it up and throw it for him to catch.

"Favorite character?" I ask, unable to stop myself from casting side glances her way.

"I'll give you one guess." She answers almost immediately with a playful tone, and I have to mentally tell myself to not look at her to check if it's still definitely Elle.

I can't fight the smile from appearing. Nodding, I realize the mistake I made. "Poe." I answer like it was obvious.

She doesn't laugh, but she lets out a little breath as her smile remains. It's genuine and pure, like freshly grown flowers once they bloom.

We wait in silence as Poe makes his return with the ball, accepting that's the end of our somewhat friendly conversation. But then her voice lights a match inside me as we make progress.

"What's yours?" She asks with a quieter voice, like she shouldn't be continuing this conversation but it's something she has genuine interest in.

"Hans." I nod, and that little breathy laugh escapes her lips again. I give in to my temptations and look at her, drinking in her appearance. Delicate freckles decorate her cheek and nose, some looking like faded petals.

"Of course." Elle's eyes flick my way. "I could've guessed that."

I'm about to ask her how she would know, but a deep voice interrupts us, pulling Elle back into her shell of safety and numbness.

"Johnny!" Kevin, a deputy, approaches me with his hand out.

Grasping his thick hand, I give a firm shake before nodding in greeting. "Kevin. How are you?"

"Good thanks, man!" He swigs his beer, which I'm certain it's illegal to have on the beach. His gaze flicks to Elle, eyes scanning up and down her side on stance. "Elle." He nods her way, but doesn't offer anything further.

Her barely visible head movement and slight smile is the only greeting she offers, before grabbing Poe's ball and giving him all her attention. Her evasion tactics are fired up straight away as she does what her protection methods tell her to do and avoids the situation.

"How's the family?" I cut the deafening silence around us in an attempt to lighten the unnerving situation. My eyes focus on Kevin as I pull his attention away from Elle.

"Ah, you know," he proceeds, to which I really don't know. "As long as she has access to my account, she's happy."

I nod, although his comment steers me further away from marriage.

"She booked a rather pricey hair appointment the other day." Kevin begins as his eyes dart between me and the back of Elle's head. "She wanted short hair like you, Elle."

Elle's head turns at the calling of her name, but she's aware of what Kevin was saying.

"Why don't you grow it? Long blonde hair would look beautiful on you." Kevin reaches his hand out to run his fingers through Elle's hair, but she instantly retracts.

Turning her eyes away from us, she shrugs her shoulders and looks at her feet. But I noticed the tears brimming on her lash line.

Kevin persists, unable to read the room. "Come on. Grow it long. It's what Stanley would want."

That comment pushes her over the edge. "I like my short hair." Elle snaps, shocking herself with her sudden outburst before shrinking into herself. She doesn't say anything further, instead she steps away and walks further down the beach with a tennis ball.

I want to close the space between me and Kevin and not so politely tell him how fucking rude he was. To never tell a woman, especially Elle, how she should look. But I can't blow my cover. And more importantly, I want to know if she's okay.

"Your wife is looking for you." I bluntly state, pointing in the general direction of the biggest crowd. Kevin curses under his breath before stomping up the stoney sand, in search of his wife.

Like deja vu, I close the few steps between me and Elle and stand next to her again. "You okay, Violet?" I question, not looking at her to make sure she doesn't feel cornered.

She just nods and doesn't offer me anything further.

I should take this as a sign to not push any further and to respect her space, but the thought of her feeling alone pierces my heart in ways I don't enjoy. I don't want her to feel vulnerable and lonely. I want her to know I'm here.

"You can trust me." The words leave my lips gently and reassuring. I keep my attention on Poe, crouching to play with him, so she doesn't feel pressured into telling me anything.

I had a fraction of hope that she would believe me, but the silence between us crushes my faith. I want to help her, but I can't when I'm steering in the dark with no headlights.

I just need a breadcrumb, the slightest clue to follow.

"Why did Kevin's comment upset you?" I pry, my tone curious but stern.

The question requests more than a simple answer. I want an explanation. A reason for her reaction.

I want to understand her.

But once again, she gives me the one thing I desperately wanted to avoid.

Her silence.

It rings loud in my ears as the pang in my chest begins throbbing. I rub my chest, worrying that something is wrong inside of me, but I know the classic symptoms of anything medical. It's not that.

It's something else.

I'm so lost in my own thoughts, trying to figure out what's happening to me, that I don't even notice Poe is bounding towards me with a ball in his mouth. He shows no signs of slowing down, and in the few seconds before he's running straight into me, my mind has a moment of realization.

Maybe Elle was telling the truth about her bruise and Poe actually did run into her. His golden colored coat moves in a flash in front of me, giving me a second to accept my fate of being knocked flat on my ass by a big teddy bear.

But the collision never comes.

Instead, Poe stops himself before he even reaches me, like it was the easiest thing he's ever done. He drops the tennis ball and waits for it to be thrown.

If he can stop himself at a speed as fast as he was going, then...

Realization wooshes the air from my lungs.

It wasn't Poe.

7

ELLE

While Sunday service is the worst part of my day, Sunday evenings are my favorite. Me and Poe are home alone, with no Stanley in sight.

I don't know what Stanley does with his time on Sunday evenings and I value my life enough not to pry, but whatever it is, it keeps him occupied until midnight.

He tells me it's a work meeting, but I know better than to believe those happen on the weekends, out of working hours. But I can't find it inside of me to care. He's out of the house and I get to relax. Like really relax.

Entering the bathroom, I check my surroundings for all the things I need. The gold and white color theme brightens the room; with a vintage design throughout, the olden style tub bath and baby cupid tiles on the wall compliment the decorated colors. Steam accumulates as boiling water runs from the taps into the bath. The scent of roses and jasmine fills the air from the bath oil as steam clouds my sight. Flames flicker around the room as the pillar candles burn slowly, each candle dotted around to create enough light for me to make out shapes and shadows.

Bringing my Kindle and a glass of pomegranate juice with me into the bathroom, I let my silk dressing gown slide down my body, leaving me bare, before hopping into the hot water. Instant goosebumps bloom over my body as the heat warms my skin, enticing me in further to feel the satisfying burn on my body.

Delicate droplets decorate my chest and arms as I lay with my back underwater, my Kindle and drink balancing on the bath tray. Rock music plays quietly on the old school radio sitting on the counter, the heavy guitars leaving me relaxed and content.

My attention focuses on the Kindle screen as a romance book is being advertised, but I'm not tempted. Romance novels leave me feeling deflated and somehow jealous of fictional characters. They have what I don't, and I hate them for it.

They have love, trust and understanding, something I could only dream about in this fucked up life.

A thriller novel pops up, reminding me of the previous book I started. From left to right, my eyes relay the words back to my brain from each sentence, but my concentration isn't as good as it usually is. I'm struggling to take in the information and make sense of the words. I'm telling my brain what my eyes are seeing, but my mind isn't allowing me to string the sentences together. Instead, it's thinking about something that shouldn't even be on my mind.

Or someone, for that matter.

Johnny's words echo on repeat in my head.

You can trust me.

It's just a passing comment, though. Right?

People don't actually mean it when they say it. It's a way to pry into others personal lives and find out their vulnerabilities.

But something tells me he isn't like other people.

Every word that leaves his lips holds meaning. Like a spoken promise, his words carry reassurance and comfort, like he'd actually be there for me instead of using my secrets as a weapon.

He feels like a confidant. *And I like it.* I like having someone there for me, wanting to know if I'm okay and what's happening in my life. Someone to listen to my worries and to tell me everything will be okay.

But is it worth it?

Once those secrets leave the safety of my lips, they're free to please anyone who comes knocking for gossip. What does he offer that shows me he'll do as he says? He's done nothing wrong, yet, I suppose. It's a better start than mine and Stanley's relationship. But what if he's the same kind of man? One who uses manipulation and gaslighting as their power tool. Then I'd have more than one monster in my life.

But is the possibility of that happening worse than my current situation? I'm living in a world of landmines that I'm convinced that's all the future holds for me. But, maybe there's another option. A chance to have someone in my corner and understand what I have to go through.

Someone to look under the bulletproof cover and see I'm still in here.

He's different in ways I can't quite decipher.

There's something inside that makes him authentic and observant. He can pick up on things that should be invisible. I've spent years perfecting my social shell for Stanley's sake, yet Johnny rips off my mask within seconds of seeing me.

No one notices, yet Johnny does.

He notices everything.

If I don't take the leap of faith and put my trust in him, he'll figure it out his own way.

I think Poe would agree with me, too, considering he actually let someone other than me throw his tennis ball, which he's very possessive over.

My mind flashes back to earlier, watching Johnny play with Poe. His gentle nature when he praised Poe for returning his ball. The words of encouragement and his soft voice. His adorable smile. And his impressive muscles as his upper arms tensed, thick veins becoming more prominent.

My thighs clench together as the pulse in between my legs throb, my eyes widening at my body's sudden reaction.

I haven't had an active sex drive since before me and Stanley got together. I thought he ruined me and I'd never enjoy sex again. I have no desire for it and Stanley only uses me to reach his own orgasm. Me, on the other hand, I sing Red Hot Chili Peppers *Under the Bridge* repeatedly until it's over so I can escape the living nightmare of his naked body, on top of me, barely moving.

But the tingling feeling crackling inside of me is awakening desires that I thought had died.

I'm still in disbelief, so I decide to test my body. It could have been a one off reaction, a slip in the moment. But as my hand trails down my torso and lands on my clit, my body enters a realm of blinding lights and bliss.

I have to inhale a deep breath to come to terms with the fire burning low in my belly. Exhaling a deep breath, I begin circling my finger, my legs widening in response. I let my head fall back and my mouth fall open, inhaling short and fast breaths as my pleasure builds inside. My freehand finds my pert nipple, flicking and soothing the sensitive skin.

My mind is solely focused on keeping a solid rhythm, perfecting it to whatever my pussy likes, but I can't stop my thoughts from trailing off. My pace picks up as I circle my clit and add more pressure, light gasps leaving my lips in response. Tattoos and muscles invade my vision, tempting the pleasure inside of me to heighten.

Stopping dead, I snap my head up and open my eyes wide. Shame hits me as I realize who was on my mind three seconds ago, edging me closer to the level of satisfaction that I haven't reached in years.

I shouldn't carry on. This is immoral and scandalous. And I should consider the fact that I'm married. Married to a man I'm not even thinking about while touching myself.

But I don't pull my hand away.

I don't allow myself to ruin the one small pleasure I have in life.

There's no one here to judge me and I'll take this to the grave. It's a secret between me and me only, and those ones I can trust will stay locked up for good.

That familiar wave of pleasure takes over my body as my head falls back and my hand begins circling again. My body is sensitive to every movement, each touch is like an electric current, leaving my body buzzing and reactive, desperate for more.

Beige skin, thick muscles, edible lips. Johnny invades my mind, like every encounter we've ever had was for this exact moment. Each mental snapshot I have of him is pulling me to blissful ecstasy.

I wonder what his hands would feel like on my pussy as they tease me. How his voice would sound as he encourages me to orgasm. How he would feel deep inside me.

The yelp escapes my lips before I can stop it.

My body tenses and releases as I'm thrown into a world of euphoria, my vision nothing but stars and the air in my lungs releasing as a shallow moan. I grind my pussy on my hand as I ride myself through the mind-blowing orgasm, soaking up as much of this high as I possibly can. My nerve endings are on fire and my body feels weightless as this addictive climax possesses me, edging me to keep going even though my body is heavy with pleasure.

Slowing my thrusts and calming my breathing, I swipe the sweat droplets from my forehead and stare forward into nothingness.

I can't believe I just did that.

Orgasms that shatter the mind are goddamn addictive.

Orgasms that are caused from the thought of someone else are sinful.

Yet, sinning never felt so tempting.

8

JOHNNY

Fury burns deep in my stomach as I piece together Elle's lies and her bruise. I guess living in a small town like Charlestown, with a tight knit group of husbands who do the work and wives who spend the money, they often look past warning signs.

I refuse to believe no one considered Elle's injury to be from a harmless accident. There has to be someone in this town who's brain isn't fucking dysfunctional to know that was given to her by a person. More than likely her husband.

Then again, she's usually glued to Stanley's side, and if he's at work, she's at home or the cafe. There aren't many opportunities for her to cross paths with a concerned citizen. She's isolated. Cautious. Untrusting. The kind of person who blends into the background and doesn't want to draw attention to herself. And it seems to work for her; she doesn't socialize at the markets and always sits next to Stanley in church. Everyone looks past her like she's a part of the scenery.

And she probably expects that's how her life is going to be. But I see her. I notice every little thing she does, from slyly giving Poe small amounts of her food when she's at the markets to touching her daisy tattoo to ground herself.

She panicked and came up with the first lie she could think of when I questioned her bruise. She didn't have an excuse prepared or a nonchalant tone about her. She fully expected no one to notice, because that's the shit hand she's been dealt.

That's why she won't tell me a single fucking thing. Because she thinks she's trapped. She thinks no one cares enough to help her and if they did, her husband holds a position of power. She's scared, powerless and defeated.

My fist pounds on the oak table in the shoebox staff room from allowing my emotions get the better of me. I lost control for a sheer second, filling me with disappointment. I have no room for slip-ups and I need to pull myself together.

But this is no longer one job of investigating Charlestown's corruptness.

It's saving Elle, too.

I'm convinced Mayor Clyde and his cronies don't even notice me anymore. I get a 'good morning' and that's it. They've stopped asking me prying questions about my personal life and everything else under the sun and have simply accepted I'm going to be around at all times.

They've even gotten comfortable enough to explain in detail who they're having affairs with and what positions they fucked in. They obviously aren't aware I already know that shit when I did intel, but it tells me more about their trust than their personal affairs. If they are willing to admit their wrongdoings in front of a man they barely know, they clearly aren't afraid of any consequences they could face. They have everything they want; money, family, power. Even if someone ran their mouth, no one would believe them. Charlestown residents aren't stupid enough to go against their authority.

Thursday afternoons are for town hall meetings, but without the town. It's simply for the police department and the councilors to discuss town improvements and town issues. Well, that's what it's supposed to be for.

I haven't had a chance to plant a listening device in the conference room so the conversations within this room have remained private, with its trusty sound proof walls and its thick door.

Until now.

Thank fuck they're no longer interested in me. I managed to discreetly plant a microphone inside a lamp base and checked the interference was minimal, before sneaking back out and getting back to work. The ear piece in my left ear is for security reasons to have the heads up if there is a threat nearby. But a speaker device, the size of a grain of rice, sits in my right ear, giving me clear audio of the conference room.

Mayor Clyde finally, but struggling, rises from his office chair and stomps towards the door as he grunts his way to the conference room. I follow closely behind, my eyes constantly assessing our surroundings for anything out of the ordinary. Comfortable and calm employees stroll around the building in their suits and briefcases, laughing and joking loudly. The scent of thick coffee fills my nostrils as the multiple coffee machines buzz around the large foyer.

Slowly making our way down the narrow hallway, Stanley appears from his office and nods to me in greeting. I nod in return and watch as he paces alongside Mayor Clyde. I try to inspect his hands for any bruises, but I'm out of luck. All I see is his gleaming gold wedding ring on his left hand, leaving me with a bitter taste in my mouth. Clenching my fists, I focus on my day job instead of the tingling feeling inside my chest.

The conference hall is placed at the back of the building where no offices are nearby. My guess is it minimizes foot traffic and employees coming down this end, only making these meetings more suspicious.

Distant chatter begins to get louder as we narrow in towards the room. I catch a glimpse of the inside, roughly fourteen men, most of them over the age of fifty, sitting around an oval oak table with papers and pens placed in front of them. Sheriff Beasley is seated to the right of the head of the table, with the head and the left seats still available. Stanley paces in first and sits opposite Sheriff Beasley, saving one free seat for Mayor Clyde, but before he enters the room, he gives me a brief nod.

As expected, the door is closed in front of me and I'm stood guarding the door, like every other weekly meeting. The hallway is so silent that I can hear my own heart beating, each slow thump in perfect rhythm.

Swiping my phone from my pocket, I turn the speaker device in my ear on and listen in to their conversations. Low, booms of laughter echo with jokes of golf and church. Constantly slating the priest and the town hall receptionists. Typical chatter from older men.

The minutes tick by with no evidence of a crime, but if there's one thing my actual job offers, it's being a private investigator teaches you to be patient. Everything is a waiting game and sometimes you are left empty handed, but sometimes you aren't. It's worth the wait to get that inch of a lead you've been so desperately waiting for.

Bile in my stomach starts to sway when the town hall attendees begin talking about their wives in dehumanizing ways. Each insult and degrading comment is responded to with a laugh, filling me with painful annoyance. Disgusting commentary explaining what positions their wives like and how they aren't getting sex as often as they used to because their wives are 'old', and it's their wives fault they have to find sex elsewhere. They actually think their wives are the reason they have gone out of their way to seek an intimate relationship elsewhere, like they don't hold any responsibility.

I recognize Sheriff Beasley's and Mayor Clyde's voice, and I almost vomit at their words. Very confidently admitting they'd happily fuck each others wives just to know if they're as pretty while getting fucked as they are at church.

Fucking scum.

My hand finds my face as I slide it down from forehead to chin, regaining some composure. I think the worst of it is done and they'll begin talking business, but I'm wrong. A familiar voice begins speaking, and I instantly know it's Stanley. I found myself silently thanking him ten seconds ago for not pitching in on that humiliating conversation, but I'm now heavy with dread.

Descriptive sex scenes are enough to enrage me, but he doesn't stop there. He's trying to get one up on the other men as he states Elle is only twenty-four and a young wife is the way to go. She's obedient, submissive and nice to look at.

Violence blurs my vision as my body burns hot, each descriptive remark fuelling my building outburst. I can barely control my rapid heart rate as my lungs fill and deflate at a sudden speed.

I try my absolute fucking hardest to compose myself, closing my eyes and calming my breathing the way I was taught in the academy. Evidence is the main goal here, and I cannot ruin it.

But it just gets worse. Stanley's brutal words play on repeat in my mind like a blaring alarm.

"She was even better at twenty-one. Young, inexperienced, easy to manipulate. Like my own goddamn sex toy."

I can't control myself anymore. Acting on the twinge inside my heart, I don't give my brain a chance to logically think before my feet are turning me around towards the door. My hand grasps the handle with a grip strong enough to kill, but I'm frozen on the spot.

"The drop is in ten days. I need you all there to help me cut and package." Mayor Clyde's voice is dripping in authority, the sudden joking man from two minutes ago gone.

My feet take me away from the door to my previous standing position as triumph overpowers my rage. I haven't forgotten what Stanley has said, and I'll teach him a painful lesson when the time is right.

But, for now, I'm keeping my mouth shut and my evidence closeby. Because we got the goddamn drop date.

Now I just need to break a few more laws to get the location.

And then I can get Elle.

9

ELLE

This week has been far from the usual, but what's made it really bizarre is Stanley suggesting I walk Poe along the beach this evening, alone. He's home and he usually likes me to be home with him, but instead, he's shooing me out the door.

I don't refuse though. In fact, I can't get my shoes on quick enough. My cream colored pumps are washed out by my white daisy dress, but fashion isn't my main concern right now. Time away from Stanley is a privilege I'm not about to pass up.

Any loving wife would be concerned by their husband's sudden change in character, but loving isn't a word I'd use to describe myself. I think repulsed is more accurate. Anything to get me an hour away from this man and this toxic household. My feet are tired from walking on constant eggshells, desperate for a smooth path without the looming fear of an outburst on its way.

Something has changed inside of me. The temptation to escape from this hell is beginning to scream so loud that it's on a constant loop in my mind. Sure, the temptation has always been there, but it's been a distant dream that had no chance of coming true. Now, I find myself wanting to face all consequences to just try and make it out safely.

I don't want this life.

Before, it was about staying out of trouble and taking the only solution offered to me.

But the possibility of someone offering a helping hand, even if it's from a man who I met barely a month ago, gives me a sense of hope and freedom. A fresh start. A possibility to be myself again. Not this drained, subservient version of myself that Stanley created.

My feet take me to Charlestown beach, the pink sunset blooming in the sky and the waves singing hushed lullabies as they crash in the distance. There's not a single soul nearby as families spend their evenings at home, soaking in the sweet evenings with their loved ones. A light breeze kisses my bare arms, goosebumps littering my skin. It's not a cold evening in Charlestown, but the beach air has a chill to it. Inwardly cursing myself for not bringing a jacket, I throw Poe's tennis ball with all the muscle I have before rubbing my arms and in a useless attempt to create some heat.

The small stones along the beachfront bounce off the front of my pumps as I make my way towards the more secluded end of the beach. The only voice I hear is my own as I praise Poe for bringing back his ball each time, along with Poe's unnecessary loud pants when he returns.

A dull ache begins consuming my upper right arm as the constant ball throwing tires it out, so I decide to swap arms. The movement feels foreign, but I proceed anyway. How hard can it be to throw a ball with your less dominant arm?

Lifting my arm upwards, I pull it back before forcing it forward with all my strength and release.

Well, that was shameful.

The tennis ball makes it barely half the length my dominant arm threw it. I'm beyond thankful no one is around to see that monstrosity.

But my right arm still aches, so I have no other choice than to throw with my left arm. I try to step into it this time as we narrow in on the secluded area, my palm releasing the fuzzy ball as it travels in the air. I can't even see where the ball landed, the throw was that bad. But Poe loves a good explore, so I leave the tennis ball hunting in his hands. Or paws.

I can no longer see his golden coat as he disappears behind the large rocks, tracking that stupid ball. I'm sure I didn't throw it *that* bad that it went the opposite way, but my throwing talents are as good as my ability to stand up for myself.

Pretty shameful.

I give him a few more seconds to try to locate the ball before I decide I'm going to help him, but before I can take a step towards him, the tennis ball goes flying past my eyes like a meteor, before landing yards away behind me.

So, tennis balls can throw themselves now? Thank god for that.

Then, a big muscular figure appears from the rocks, dressed in a figure hugging white t-shirt that shows off his toned abs and thick arms, and gray joggers, with that familiar tattoo sleeve on his arm.

Johnny.

His oak brown eyes dart to mine and his cheeks lift as that gentle smile appears. "Beautiful evening for a stroll." His soft voice carries over the waves in the background like a sweet song.

I nod, unable to stop my lips from giving the smallest smile. "If you ignore the awful sand, the beach is pretty decent." My eyes scan my surroundings to make sure the beach is still deserted, the instant relief calming me when I notice it is.

Johnny's eyes squint behind me, looking around for something. "No Stanley?" He questions, his attention back on me.

"Not tonight." I respond, trying to keep my tone from sounding happy. "Just me and Poe."

Poe begins running back towards us, and I wait for him to bring his ball to me to throw it again, but he runs over to Johnny, instead. Dropping the ball in front of him, Johnny chuckles before picking up the ball and throwing it nearly half way down the beach. I try not to stare at him, but I can't pull my eyes away from his arm when he throws the ball. Strong muscles contracting, each groove and curve visible on his toned arm. Like he was personally sculpted, my eyes gaze down to his clothed body, wondering if the rest of him is as eye pleasing as his arm. Memories of the bathtub come to mind, and I'm sucked into a pleasant daydream.

"So," Johnny pulls me from my daze, my body jumping back to the present and my eyes snapping up to his. A lucky escape as his eyes remain on Poe, somehow not catching me in the act. "What brings you out tonight?" His inquiry is a passing question, no hint of curiosity or prying.

"Stanley said-" I zip my mouth shut. Frantically thinking of a normal excuse, I search my suddenly foggy brain for an answer. "Stanley has a business meeting at our home. I didn't want to impose." My fingers find each other as I nervously twiddle them at my near slip up. I'm too scared to look at Johnny, in case he can see through my lies on my fear driven body.

"You can't impose in your own home, Violet." he chuckles, and I'm almost certain it's a joke, but uncertainty still sits at the forefront of my mind.

"Poe needed a walk, too." I can feel the defense coating my tone.

"He's a sweet boy." He bends to stroke Poe as he grasps the tennis ball. "When did you get him?"

A sigh of relief leaves my lips. A topic that doesn't include me and Stanley. "Three and a half years ago. It was my last day at Pineridge University and we took a class trip to the local pound. He was barely six months, sitting so patiently waiting for someone to take him home. I fell in love the second I saw him." My mind flashes back to that day when I was carefree and enjoying my life. Surrounded by friends, soaking up all that college life could offer. "His previous owners gave him up because he was too energetic," I say in quotations. "He's been nothing but a blessing for me."

"Sounds like a perfect match." Johnny coos. I don't realize the gap between us has gotten smaller as Poe brings the ball back in between us, forcing one of us to move closer to the other. "Seems like you're inseparable."

My gaze falls on him, his eyes already on me. I can't help but squint, curious as to what that means, but I don't get a chance to ask.

"You take him everywhere with you. The beach, the markets," he pauses. "The cafe." His gaze doesn't waver. Instead, his eyes are glued to me, studying my reaction.

My stomach drops. My fear is about to come true and Johnny is going to blackmail me with that stupid secret. I can barely keep my face in check as my breathing picks up, hands shaking with anticipation as it fills me with the pending offer he's going to force onto me.

Johnny's eyebrows drop and his smile dissipates. Concern fills his features, his hands shooting up in defense. "Elle, I'm not going to use it against you." He seems unsure with his statement, like he's worried he's going to say the wrong thing.

I want to believe him. I have no reason not to believe him, he's kept the secret under wraps for me, as far as I know. But I have no reason to trust him, either.

Awful possibilities attack my mind as I sink into a mental room of fight or flight. Logical thoughts are so far out the window that the only thing I'm worried about is how to protect myself from this power play. My heart thumps painfully hard, the chaotic rise and fall of my chest causing my ears to throb.

This really is the worst case scenario, and I'm sinking in quicksand with no rescue team ready to help.

"Elle." Warm hands grasp my arms, yanking me from my panicked mind back to the present. But it doesn't feel much safer here, either. "Hey." Johnny's tone is sharp, causing my wide eyes to meet his. "I'm not going to do anything to put you in danger, Elle. Is this how you live every day?" Worry is etched on his face, his brows pulled together as his eyes widen.

His question catches me off guard, pausing me on the spot and unable to recoil from his touch. It's gentle. Reassuring. *Humane.*

I try to decipher his worrying reaction, trying to piece together ways he can use this against me. Trying to figure out his game plan. But my mind is all jumbled and disconnected. It's too focused on Johnny's words.

I'm not going to do anything to put you in danger.

The opportunity sits like a stationary boat in front of me, ready for me to take the leap and sail away. To take a chance on myself and give myself a shot at a normal life. It's giving me the opportunity to put my trust in someone else, with the optimistic chance they'll save me.

But doubt is a shadowy figure in the corner, looming over the door to scare my opportunity away. Frightening me to stay in bed where I'm comfortable, not allowing me the chance to escape.

I have two choices. Let my nightmares scare me into staying in this fearsome life. Or push past them and run for a lightswitch.

I choose the lightswitch.

"What you said the other day." My voice is barely a whisper as unease sinks my body. "Can I really trust you?" My body automatically takes a step back out of Johnny's grip, his hands releasing me.

"Of course." He nods. Concern still sits on his face as his shoulders tense. He doesn't tower over me. Instead, he takes a step back to a lower area of pebbles so his eyeline matches mine. "You're safe with me, Violet."

I ignore the pleads of refusal in the back of my mind and take a deep breath to center myself, my eyes closing as I do so. "I'm not with Stanley out of love." The confession leaves my lips, confused how I feel like a weight has been lifted off my shoulders. It feels good to admit the truth, for once.

"I figured that." Johnny sighed, somewhat looking defeated.

"He has something on me that could ruin my future career and I can't risk that. It's my only chance to get out of this marriage." I scoff. "If that's even possible."

Johnny shakes his head. "What does he have on you?" He must sense my hostility as he takes a deep breath. "You don't have to tell me if you aren't comfortable."

He's not prying for answers or giving me ultimatums. It almost feels foreign to have someone give me control and space to explain myself in my own time.

"He caught me stealing in a convenience store when I was twenty-one and used his authority to scare me into marriage." I shrug, knowing exactly what it sounds like. She's a thief, she deserves this life. "It was ramen noodles and aspirin." I clarify, a humorless laugh leaving my lips. "My mother died in my third, and final, not my choice but Stanley's, semester at college. She had some debts to her name and once she passed, I spent all my money paying them off. I was left with nothing. I had one year left of college and I never even got to complete it." Tears brim my eyes, my past being a constant reminder of where I am now. "I had no choice."

"I'm so sorry, Elle. That must have been really hard for you." His sympathy wraps around me like a warm blanket, giving me comfort and understanding.

"She wasn't a bad woman. She was a single mother who was living on a florist's wage in small town Charlestown. It was hard to make ends meet, and the only way to keep our home was to take out loans. Unfortunately, the cancer took her before I could help."

My sight is blurred with salty tears as they fall down my cheeks. Clenching my eyes shut, I try to clear my vision, but arms wrap around me, soothing my pain and offering comfort. I should push him off me, but I don't want to. This is the safest I've felt since I met Stanley, I'm allowing myself to bask in it for a little longer.

Mandarin and leather invades my nostrils as his scent offers solace. A safe landing place.

I can't help but feel like he's pitying me though. I know why I'm in this situation and I know I'm not escaping it anytime soon. It's something I just have to deal with. "I don't want your pity." I croak. Taking a step back to create space.

"I'm not pitying you, Elle. I'm comforting you. There's a difference." Johnny follows my lead and takes a step back so he can see me. I'm not exactly happy he can see my tear streaked cheeks, but at least it's safer than someone catching us mid-hug and the word getting back to Stanley. "Has it always been bad?" He questions, a sharp toned voice.

I shake my head. "No. Our marriage started off fine. Stanley was somewhat nice to me. But he laid down his rules of my housewife duties early on. I knew from then on, he didn't see me as his equal. I was his play toy." I let out a scoff. "The first time I told him I wanted to study, he threw my study book clean across the room. In an instant, he turned it around on me, saying *I'm* the reason he's acting out because I'm trying to be smarter than him." The lump in my throat makes it harder for me to get my words out, but I try and power on. If I stop now, I may never start again. "He's convinced I want to study so I can leave him. No consideration of my future career, the reason I went to college, what I want to accomplish in life. In our house, the only way is Stanley's way. And he's scary when he doesn't get what he wants." The words leave my lips like a threat. I suppose it is a threat, but directed at me.

Yet, it felt good to finally tell someone the truth.
The hellhole that's my life.

10

JOHNNY

I don't want to scare Elle, so my exterior is kept calm, but that doesn't ease the blazing anger flooding every inch of my body. I'm certain she hasn't told me the full extent of what she goes through on a daily basis, but I've heard enough to know this man deserves to be put down.

Her tense body and jumpy reactions tell me everything I need to know. She's fucking scared of this man. He literally holds her future in his hands like a water balloon, and any time she decides to stick up for herself, he squeezes, threatening to burst and ruin everything. All over a packet of ramen.

After all Elle's hard work attending college, this is the future she's given. One where she's on a constant schedule, having to do all the dirty work for a lazy, old bastard. A maid in her own home, except, she doesn't get the luxury of her shift ending. Instead, she has to do as she's told, cook every single meal and share the same goddamn bed with this man.

The thought makes my jaw clench.

A breathtaking sunset and not a single soul in sight, yet I can't focus on the gorgeous scenery. I'm too busy memorizing each word Elle says, all while trying to contain the bizarre swelling feeling in my chest.

A thought crosses my mind as I remember Elle's reaction to a single comment. "The hair," I nod towards her own. "What really upset you about Kevin's comment?" I try to push her for answers, even though her uncomfortable position makes me feel like a dick.

I need all the information so I know how to protect her.

Sky blues meet my eyes, a sea of emotion swimming in them. Her eyebrows pull together as her mouth opens, but she quickly snaps it shut. "It's stupid," Elle waves off, letting a scoff leave her lips.

"Hey." I close the gap between us to grasp her upper arm, rubbing up and down her soft skin for reassurance. I don't miss her flinch, but she relaxes as I retract my hand. "Nothing you say or do is stupid, Violet. You have no similarities with that word."

A long pause surrounds us, and I give Elle all the time in the world for her to feel comfortable. "He used to pull me back by my hair if I walked away from him. I decided to take that power away from him." Tears brim her lash line, but they don't fall. Instead, they create the prettiest ocean I've ever seen.

My tongue swipes along my teeth as I fight the urge to clench my jaw. Seething hatred builds inside me towards Stanley, but it's balanced with a drowning ache for Elle. I loathe him for how he treats her, but the urge to protect Elle fights harder inside of me.

"I'm guessing he didn't take that well." My tone is detached, silently pleading Elle's answer isn't as bad as I know it to be.

"Nonstop insults and a lot of emotional belittling. He didn't lay a hand on me, though." She must have noticed the slight dip in my brows. "I know that's what you're thinking."

Flashbacks to Elle's bruised cheek infiltrate my mind. "But he has."

Squinting back at me, she tilts her head sideways, as if she's unsure of my statement.

"Laid a hand on you." I clarify. I swear I see fear in her eyes, like I've sussed out her big secret. My finger flicks between us, "this is trust." I tell her, hoping to reassure her. I ignore the pang in my chest that tells me she isn't sure of me. If only she knew how often I think about her.

"It was once." The words spill from her lips like a lifeline, her tear filled lash line finally following the path of previous droplets.

"That fucking-" I don't get to finish my sentence because she cuts me up to defend that prick.

"It's not something that happens regularly and he promised it wouldn't happen again. He had a bad day at work and-"

"Elle." I cut her words off, unable to hear her defend the man who hurt her. "There is no one to blame other than Stanley himself. A stressful job doesn't mean you hit your wife. He is the problem, not you." Instant regret floods me as she starts balling, sobs escaping her lips as she tries to inhale as much air as she can get.

I want to pull her close to my chest and give her the comfort she needs. A safe space for her to let out her emotions while not fearing an aggressive reaction. But I don't want to push her barriers, so I settle for grasping her hands. Despite her sunken shoulders and impending sadness, her touch is warm and soothing.

"It's because I overcooked the duck." She laughs but there's nothing funny about her statement. "His frustration got the better of him and he stepped on Poe's tail by accident. Poe, reacting like any dog would, tried to run and knocked over a glass. It just added more gasoline to Stanley's burning fire." Her voice restricts as her eyes glance to Poe, who's resting on an area of pebbles. "He wanted to punish Poe but I could never allow that. I'll take the hit for him every single time."

Fuck, I wanted her close, to take every ounce of pain away. I'd carry her agony on my back so she could experience pure happiness, like she deserves.

"But it won't happen again." Elle interrupts my thoughts, my gaze falling on her fragile state. "He promised."

"Promises mean nothing when there isn't mutual respect. It's just verbal assurance to get them what they want." I see the devastation sink in her eyes and it breaks my fucking heart.

She needs security, something that she can hold onto and know there's hope for the future. Something that tells her there's more to life than just surviving.

I pull her close to my body, but she flinches and instantly recoils. Her eyes dart around our surroundings, the sunset dipping below the sea line and the beach deserted. It's a stab in the heart to know she's always this worried to be caught, from fear of what Stanley might do.

"There's something you need to know." The words come from my lips quieter than my usual tone.

"Have you-" Elle pauses, her darting eyes around us trying to figure something out. "Is this a trap?" She questions, almost accepting her fate.

"No, Violet. I would never do that to you." I know she doesn't hear me when I say she can trust me, but I won't stop reassuring her. I'll say it until she believes it. "Your husband is under investigation for drug trafficking."

Pinched eyebrows and squinted eyes tell me she had no clue what Stanley was actually doing at work. "How do you know this?"

"Because I'm the private investigator on the case."

Fear flashes across her face, her gaze widening as she steps back urgently. The rise and fall of her chest picks up its pace, her hand pressing against her chest to ease her breathing. "Does that mean-" Elle gulps, tears filling her lash line once again. "Does that mean you're using me to get answers?"

Devastation fills her expression and I swear I feel my heart crack at her appearance. "Of course not. I would never use my position or real reason for being here against you, Elle. I meant it when I said you can trust me." Attempts to reassure her fall flat as she seems immersed in her own worrisome mind.

"Oh my god, I'm so stupid." That humorless laugh makes another appearance. "I told you I stole!"

"Elle, I'm not here to investigate you. I couldn't give a shit if you told me you murdered someone." I try to reach for her again, and to my surprise, she doesn't recoil this time. I pull her close enough that our faces are inches apart. I can see the small crease between her eyebrows, and how prominent her cupid's bow is. "I'm investigating the council and the police department. Finding out what Stanley does to you is just more of a reason to throw his ass in jail."

Elle's mouth is open slightly as she looks everywhere but my actual face. "Promise you aren't going to use your power to manipulate me, just like Stanley did?" The words are soft and vulnerable as her cheeks flush a light shade of pink.

"There are absolutely no similarities between me and that sick son of a bitch." The words slip from my mouth before I can stop them, but I'm not sorry I said them. They're nothing but the truth. "But I'm undercover, so, if it's okay with you, I need you to keep my identity a secret." I'm playing with fire by risking my job. I'm in deep shit if this goes tits up.

She finally looks at me and the air whooshes from my lungs. Her gaze can convince me to do anything. The thought raises alarm bells in my mind as I realize how far I'd go for this girl, but I don't let them scare me away.

Raising her pinky up, she waits patiently, with a sweet smile on her face. I grip her delicate finger with my own, wrapping them around each other. Her cheeks lift as her eyes twinkle, and I actually see the tension in her shoulders finally dissipate.

She feels safe enough to relax.

That thought alone gives me butterflies.

Fucking butterflies.

It feels like a bubble envelops us as our surroundings blur away. I can't hear the sea or the wind, and I can't see anything other than this goddess in front of me. All I can focus on is the low thump of my racing heart rate, how mesmerizing her rose and jasmine scent is, and the warmth radiating from her delicate skin.

She has me hypnotized, not a single thing could distract me from this moment in time. My logical thinking is out of the window when my eyes are focused on her pink plump lips, desperate to find out how they taste.

Edging forward, I hear her breathing pick up, but she doesn't pull away, I move closer, so close that I can feel her warm breath against my lips. The gap between us is so minute, yet I don't feel close enough to her.

Fuck it. I'm taking the risk.

I close the gap so our lips brush against each other, and the slight touch shoots electricity through my body, filling me with anticipation and temptation.

But I don't push further. I want to give Elle the option to pull away if she doesn't feel comfortable. She needs to know the ball is in her court and I'm not here to overpower her. She's in charge. For once in her goddamn life.

And she takes control, making the choice for herself.

Skin against skin, fire against gasoline. Our lips collide, so gentle yet filled with ecstasy. Cherry invades my taste buds as passion builds between us, my hands finding her cheeks as our kiss has no end time.

Her arms snake around my waist as her fingers trace the ridges of my back, her touch tender yet compelling. Each second her skin is touching my body, desire fights its way from that buried spot inside of me to the forefront of my mind, awakening every nerve inside of me. It's telling me to deepen the kiss and have her flush against me, but the captivating moment between us is cut short.

Sudden ringing from Elle's pocket pulls us back to reality, instant devastation smacking me in the face. If sixteen year old me could see me standing on the beach with a fucking boner from a kiss, he'd be rinsing me with insults right now. I reposition myself so the bulge in my pants isn't obvious, and pray to fucking god that it goes down soon.

We step apart and create a gap between us, only a few inches, but the space already leaves a pit in my stomach. Elle scrambles to find her phone and pulls it out, sighing before answering.

I can't hear who she's speaking to, but her obedient responses and tense shoulders tells me it's Stanley. "I didn't realize the time. I went the long route to tire him out." Her hush tone and apologies fall so easily from her lips, for a man who doesn't deserve a single thing from her. "Yeah, I'll be right home."

"Sorry." Apologies now directed at me as she locks her phone and places it into her pocket. "I have to go."

"Don't apologize, Violet." I can't help but pick up on her features, her sunken eyes and sad smile. "Need a ride?" I ask, nodding the way to my car.

She pauses for a second and then glances at Poe. "It's okay. No dogs in the car." A statement instead of a question.

I squint at her. "Says who? He's allowed in my car." I reassure her, grasping my car keys from my pocket.

"Stanley doesn't allow him in his car so I understand if you don't either." She steps away from me towards Poe, and each step feels like a punch in the gut. A step towards danger, when her protection lays in her hands. She gently strokes Poe to wake him up, and with a big stretch and a yawn, he gets up on his feet, but slumps back down straight after.

"Yeah, you aren't walking." I smile towards Poe. "Come on, buddy!" I whistle, and sure enough, Poe is up, albeit begrudgingly, and starts following us.

A short thirty second walk to the car and I encourage Poe into the boot of my black Land Rover as Elle watches over me. That dog really is her sanity.

I shut the boot and guide Elle around to the passenger side and open the door for her. I take her hand as she takes the big step into the passenger seat, before shutting the door behind her.

I waste no time hopping in and starting the car. I'm conscious of how long it takes her to get home, because I don't want to give that bastard a reason to hit her again. I'd kill him if he ever laid a finger on her again.

I don't ask for directions, and she doesn't bother giving me any. There's no point, considering I know where she lives anyway. The air-con hums as the radio plays on low volume in the background, filling the silence surrounding us.

Pushing Elle right now is the last thing I want to do. I don't need her thoughts or an explanation for what just happened between us. I don't want to be another problem in her life that causes her anxiety.

"Can you drop me at the corner?" Elle's barely audible voice pulls me from my thoughts. "It's just," she pauses. "If Stanley sees me getting out of a car that isn't mine, he'd lose his mind."

"Of course." I nod, narrowing in on the corner. I'm thankful for the darkness inside of the car so Elle can't see how furious her statement makes me.

The car comes to a slow stop as I pull up against the sidewalk, before hopping out and making it around to her door while she's still unbuckling. "You know where I live." Elle states plainly, trying to mask a smile. "You really take this PI thing seriously."

"It's my job." I wink, holding my hand out for her to grasp. That familiar electric shock zaps my arm as our hands clasp, but I release her hand as soon as her grip loosens. Popping open the trunk, I let Poe hop out, giving him a quick rub before he walks over to Elle.

I watch each step she takes further away from me, silently cursing myself for letting her go back to that house. "Elle." I shout, her back turning as soon as the word leaves my mouth. "Stay safe."

"I'll try." She says with a smile, although I see the fear within her eyes.

I hop back into my car before I let my anger get the better of me, but I watch until she enters her house safely. Lights flicker on and I see her through the window as she hangs Poe's lead up. She disappears from my sight, but I spot her again as she enters a dim lit office. She flicks the main light on and I see Stanley sat at his desk, working on his computer. They speak for a minute, and the conversation seems calm. I release a breath.

Starting my car, I check my mirrors to make sure it's safe to pull away, but my gaze is pulled to Elle, who's now upstairs in her home. She's standing at the window in front of a mirror, her curtains open, and she starts undressing.

My cock twitches from the sheer thought of knowing I've touched even a precious inch of that gorgeous skin. My hand finds its way to my cock, and the temptation to touch myself is so fucking strong. But I'm not allowing myself to do that to her. So, I force the car in drive and pull away, far away from the girl who's plagued my thoughts and far away from the risque temptation that claws at my chest.

I'm not doing that to her. Objectifying her would make me just as bad as Stanley.

Flashbacks from our kiss flood my mind, making driving home with a fucking everlasting boner that much harder. The feeling is unfamiliar to me. I've never had the desire to put my work aside and focus on a woman. I've never had a relationship that lasted longer than two months, before. Hell, I've never even been in love.

Yet here I am, infatuated by a woman who isn't even available.

She's an addiction, and I should've known that one taste would be enough to pull me in.

11

JOHNNY

A clear head when heading to work used to be the norm for me, but my head hasn't been clear since last night. Like a repeating video, mine and Elle's kiss replays over and over in my mind. I feel an overwhelming desire to feel those precious lips against mine again. I want to know what the rest of her skin feels like against my lips. How her soft moans ring in my ears like a fucking lullaby.

My fists clench as I try to reel myself back into a sane head-space. Anger rises inside of me, but it's directed at myself. I shouldn't be thinking these dirty thoughts about her. I'm a man who wants to fuck the woman who is going through hell.

But the thing with hell is it's the lowest place a person can go. There isn't a worse place, but there are places that are far fucking better. And I'm going to burn hell to the ground, just so I can give Elle a piece of heaven, like she deserves.

I'm a sick bastard, but I'm human. I would never act on those desires unless she wanted me to. The fact those desires have even awakened in me have made me feel...*normal*. There's something inside of me that wants to feel passion, and I can't let that opportunity go to waste.

It may have taken half an hour of waiting my erection out, and then giving in shamefully to jerk off, but I finally got it out of my system. I couldn't have sexual frustration ruining today. Especially when I overheard Mayor Clyde mention 'drop' this morning when he thought no one was in the building.

But I awoke early and took the opportunity to come to work early, in hopes of a lead. And it was placed in front of me like dinner on a fucking table.

Wasting no time, I sneak into the mayor's office and place a listening device behind one of his kids trophies, before exiting and testing the device. There's no interference, and it's picking up good signals, so I take a quick exit out the back door to set up my phone. Activating the device, I set my phone to record and slide it back into my pocket.

I fucking hope I get something today. I need this. Elle needs this.

With forty-five minutes to spare until my shift starts, I drive over to the police department and park out of sight from any cameras, before pulling out a pocket knife and slicing my own tire. Quickly grabbing my spare tire, I swap them over and placed the slashed one in my boot. At least this one is brand new, so they'll fall for the lie I'm about to tell.

Grabbing a second listening device, I slip it into my pocket before jogging over to the cream brick building with numerous cop cars stationed outside.

Pushing open the heavy wooden door, I'm faced with a cloud of heat. Clearly they don't know how to work the fucking air-con. Desks are dotted around, stacked with paperwork and used mugs. A phone rings in the distance, but no one seems to answer it as it continues on and on. The scent of coffee fills the muggy air and popular seventies hits play on a retro radio in the corner.

It's early, so I wasn't expecting a lot of staff around. One woman sits at the front desk, her glasses propped on the bridge of her nose and her short, dark curls nearly cover her eyes. She hums to the radio, not noticing I'm standing in front of her.

I clear my throat, and she instantly lifts her eyes from her computer. "Can I help you?" She questions, her tone condescending.

"I'd like to report a crime." I answer. She moves her head down slightly as her eyebrows dart up, waiting for me to continue. "Someone slashed my tire. I had a spare so I can still drive, but I'd like to report it so it's on the record." I answer, my hands interlocked with one another as they rest on the desk.

"Follow me." She rises from her chair and grunts as she begins walking down a hallway, I follow, my eyes subtly glancing into offices and staff rooms. The place is dead, without a single soul in sight.

My eyes immediately dart to the golden plaque with 'Sheriff Beasley' written on it. The door is closed, but I don't see a keyhole.

"Take a seat, I'll grab a report." She says so quietly I barely hear her, but I see her arm pointing towards the room next to Sheriff Beasley's office, so I follow her instructions and take a seat.

She begins hobbling away, down the hallway we just walked down and begins down another corridor on the other side of the police department.

I'm not one to let opportunities pass by, so I dart up to my feet and double check the hallway is clear before stepping outside Sheriff Beasley's door. I place my ear against the cool wood as I listen for any sounds. Typing, breathing, speaking, anything. But it's silent, so I push down the handle and gently open the door.

I'm instantly hit with the scent of beer and cigarettes as my eyes gaze around the room, looking for a perfect spot. Filing cabinets covering one wall, with a large floor length window covering the wall opposite. A TV sits in the right corner, which means that corner is out of use. A coffee machine in the other, ruining my opportunity for that corner, too. I focus on the paintings behind the desk, abstract art with red, white and blue colors.

Perfect.

I lift one off its nail and notice the brown string that holds the nail up. My hand dives into my pocket and pulls out the listening device, and I quickly attach it to the string. Double checking it's on, I reattach the painting to the wall and dart towards the door, closing it behind me. Distant grunts reverberate down the hall, so I quickly take a seat in the room I was told to sit in. Glancing at my phone, I set up the listening device, before setting it to record.

Finally allowing myself a deep breath, I place my phone back in my pocket and grab myself a cup of water from the water dispenser. Each sip is each step the desk clerk takes down the hallway, and as soon as I finish my drink, she arrives at the door with a sheet of paper and a black pen.

"Fill this out and then return it to me at the front desk."

I don't even get a chance to thank her, she's too busy getting as far away from me as possible.

Rude.

I lie my way through the report, making up fake details to make it as believable as possible. I know how police departments work; they won't even bother chasing it up, so I know I can bullshit this whole report without worrying they'll drop by my apartment.

I sign off the report and pass it back to the desk clerk, who doesn't even look up at me. Heading towards the door, I stop on the spot and turn to face her. She acts like I'm not even here. I clear my throat again, and she doesn't bother to lift her head, only her eyes. "It wouldn't kill you to smile." I wink at her mockingly, before heading out the door.

I wish I could see her irritated reaction, but my shift starts in ten minutes and if there's one thing I always am, it's punctual.

My skin itches with impatience, desperate to listen to the footage I've gathered. My boss is waiting for a big break, and because of the mayor and sheriff's connections, taking them down will slash a gaping hole in their whole operation, ruining every aspect of their illicit drug trade.

I'm right there with my boss. Charlestown's corruption has been a case we've had our eye on for a long time, but every time we send an investigator out to scope out the situation, the mayor has either been too suspicious to let anything slip, or the sheriff has figured them out. That's why I've been pulled from my usual high level cases to investigate a small town. None of the newer investigators could crack this town, so instead, I'm going to rip them bare and expose them. Force the compelling evidence down their throats when they go to court.

But for tonight, I have to play into their game and pretend I'm just a small town security guard, needing a few beers after his shift. The Boathouse diner sits on Charlestown's sea front; a beach hut themed square building, with a bar on the back wall, canopies outside the windows and outdoor seating on a decking area. A large surfboard is placed on the wooden wall with locals signatures on it and upbeat music plays throughout the surrounding speakers. I scoped this place out when I was learning the town, not knowing it would be such an important location. I would've hid a few devices if I knew.

This evening is the In-House Jefe Event. The police department staff and the mayor's office staff are invited to an evening of food, drinks, and calmness. But as I sit in my car, parked further up the seafront, I notice there's not a lot of attendees. In fact, the only people sitting inside are the exact same men who attend the weekly Thursday meeting. The ones who are supposed to discuss this town's future, yet talk about anything but.

Anticipation fills low in my gut as I sense this evening isn't what it's supposed to be. The men inside are suspicious, and if they're off duty drinking beer, a few deep secrets may slip loose. I set my phone to record, just in case, before stepping out of my car and making it towards The Boathouse.

Roars and cheers erupt as I push the door open, some policemen playing pool while the other men stand by the bar or the open sliding doors, beers in one hand and cigars in the other. I nod to the less important men as I pass them and grab a beer as I pass the bar. Grabbing my wallet to pay, the young, brunette bartender waves me off, telling me it's on a tab.

Of course it is, because the men in power within Charlestown have money to burn.

Firm hands clasp my shoulders, making me tense instantly. "Hey, Johnny!" I recognize the gravelly voice instantly.

"Stanley." I nod to greet him.

Resting his elbow on the bar, he waves his hand to get the bartender's attention and points at the draft tap he wants. As she walks away to get a glass, he leans over the bar and eyes her up and down. "Fine piece of ass, huh?" He scoffs, his grin borderline predatory.

I have to bite back an insult and take a deep breath before responding. I try find a response that would satisfy him, but all that claws up my throat are statements of how fucking amazing his wife is, and how he doesn't deserve to breathe the same air as her. So instead, I just nod.

The bartender places his beer in front of him and walks off, but Stanley doesn't miss the opportunity to gawk at her again. "Damn," he shakes his head as he turns away, his eyes set on the crowd outside. "I'd tap that."

Fucking scum.

"Come on," his large hand wraps around my shoulder. "Grab your beer, we're going outside."

Grabbing my beer off the side, I quickly slide my phone from my pocket, double checking its recording before following behind him. He grunts with each step and has a slight limp on his right leg, and I fight the urge to trip him up so his other leg can hurt, too.

"Johnny's here!" Stanley announces with a croak, before coughing into his hand.

Cheers and whistles announce my arrival, with guys coming up to me, one after the other, and greeting me with a handshake or a pat on the back.

I play into their charade, even forcing a smile on my face and matching their enthusiasm, so they deem me as trustworthy. I take a seat around a circular wooden table and make myself comfy as Sheriff Beasley takes a seat next to me and Mayor Clyde shuffles a deck of cards. A small stack is placed in front of me, and it doesn't take me long to realize we are playing crazy eights.

We go a few rounds, each player fully immersed in the game that they don't take the time to judge their opponents expressions. Rule number one of card games, always bluff. Rule number two, facial expressions tell you everything.

I place my last card down and sip my beer as I revel in the fourth win. It's no fun playing with men who can't see a threat placed right in front of them. They are so focused on keeping their pathetic drug ring running, they don't realize they've let in a rat, and I'm going to sing like a fucking canary when the timing is right.

"Johnny, again!" Mayor Clyde lightly throws his cards down on the table, totaling to thirty. A solid loss.

"How are you so good at this?" Sheriff Beasley leans back in his chair, eyeing me up as amber glows at the end of his cigar.

"My father was a good teacher." I respond, keeping my answer vague so I don't have to go into details.

Relief washes over me when they don't press any further and focus on reshuffling. Going into depth about my family is the main thing I avoid when investigating, from fear of threat heading my family's way. Well, the one member left of it. Men never like when their masculinity is diminished by another man, especially when they realize they trusted the wrong person.

But going into the details of my family is a conversation I avoid with anyone. It's hard to explain your father went on a murdering spree when your mother died, and was on death row for years until he finally died a year ago. Luckily, me and my sister, Indie, haven't had to grow up feeling excluded. Our names were left out of news reports and our grandparents moved us away straight after it happened. At eight years old, I was old enough to remember the chaos that was happening back then, but my little sister was only one year old. I'm glad she was young, so she didn't have to experience the loss and confusion I felt when it all went down.

Our once full table is now occupied with half the amount of people as the others head off for beer top ups and to use the bathroom. Stanley hands me a cigar but I refuse.

"Not a smoker?" He questions, shoving it back into its packet.

"Not a cigar smoker." I confirm, sipping on the watered down beer.

"Do you smoke cigarettes?" Mayor Clyde asks as he leans back in his chair, mansplaining, while he struggles to light his cigar.

"Nope." I deadpan.

"Drugs?" Sheriff Beasley questions. A laugh is on the tip of my tongue, but when I look at him, he's deadly serious with a straight face and beady eyes.

"No, sir." I wipe my hands down my thighs and readjust my sitting position. This conversation is so fucking boring, it could put me to sleep.

Sheriff Beasley leans closer, his arm resting on the edge of my chair. I can smell the tobacco on his breath, somehow this asshole has been inhaling the cigar smoke. "I'm off duty. You can tell me if you do drugs." His eyes have a wicked glint to them, like anything he says, he'll do the opposite.

"I don't do drugs." I answer bluntly, but offering a light smile. I shouldn't overstep, but the temptation is bubbling inside of me. "Do you?" I ask, matching his raised eyebrow and smirk.

His smile is smacked off his face as he leans back and glares at me. If looks could kill, I'd be joining my father in the ground. But then a loud bellow echoes from his chest as he smacks his leg. "I don't." He shrugs, passing a quick glance to Stanley and Mayor Clyde like he's silently asking permission. They both return his devilish grin. "I know a few young girls who do, though. We sell them the best smack in the state. They're a good fuck, too."

Fucking bingo.

My expression is neutral, but my insides are burning with succession. Three sentences and they've signed their own fucking jail sentence.

But it's not enough.

"Oh yeah?" I entice them, leaning forward with a smug smile plastered on my face. "Who's we?" I press. "Room for one more?"

"Me, Stanley, Clyde, the rest of the men here. We run the operation and share the stakes." Sheriff Beasley's back hand lands on Mayor Clyde's chest. "What do you think, brother? We got room for one more?"

Mayor Clyde's eyes travel down my chest, sizing me up, before meeting my eyes. "I think we do."

A fool can be fooled again, especially when their sight is set on greed. Their own selfishness is what ends up drowning them in the end...and there's always bigger fish in the sea to show them they're the bottom of the food chain.

12

ELLE

My lips have been tingling since Johnny kissed me a few nights ago. The sensation is a constant reminder of the grass being greener on the other side, but there's a giant river in between us with no boat to sail across.

Butterflies are on a constant racing track, fluttering around my body the second he invades my mind, and the memory of his warm body flush against mine makes my lower belly ache with need.

Yet, I feel like a traitor. I may not agree with my marriage to Stanley, but I have a ring on my finger which basically screams I'm off the market. I made a legal commitment, and I'm just as bad as him to break my vows.

Even if it's something I've thought about doing almost every single fucking day of our marriage. It doesn't mean I have the balls to act on it, though.

I *shouldn't* have acted on it. I gave into temptation and it took me through a whirlwind of visions of what my life *could* be like. But could is a possibility. An indefinite in life. And I don't need to be jumping into any more situations that can't offer me a life worthy of living. I've wasted too much time existing, being an object for a man who doesn't understand respect. I won't allow myself to fall into that trap again.

Stanley didn't return home last night, but I can't find an inch of worry inside of me. I'll go to hell for thinking it, but a part of me hopes he fell in the sea or choked on his own vomit. At least I'd be free of his existence.

I had a whole bed to myself, and I even let Poe jump up and join me. Contentment consumed me knowing Stanley's bloated hands weren't going to snake around my waist in the night. Instead, I had a ball of golden fluff taking the spot as little spoon, while I nuzzled into Poe.

I glance at the alarm clock as the red light flickers six in the morning. I should be rolling out of bed to make Stanley's breakfast, so I decide to stick to routine and still make my own, just in case he waltzes through the door. Letting the bagels brown in the oven, I quickly dash upstairs and step into a gorgeous rose pink midi dress, clipping half of my hair up in a claw clip before lighting dabbing on some makeup.

Laying the table with a cotton white cloth, I place my plate in front of my chair and grab myself a glass of pomegranate juice. My teeth cut into the lightly salted avocado, the light nutty flavor relishing on my taste buds. Light ticks from the grandfather clock echo down the hallway, and I glance at the time. Nine o'clock in the morning. Stanley definitely isn't coming home. Considering he prioritizes work more than anything in his life, he'd be at the office by now.

A ping of excitement rushes through me as I soak in all the time I've had at home, alone. It feels like a fever dream, a life alone with just me and Poe, yet the doom of Stanley still being in our lives is weighing on my shoulders.

But I don't allow myself to think that way. Instead, I dig deep and muster the courage to do something I've never had the guts to do before.

Study at home.

My safe keeping vent is pried open as I gather my study books and pastel highlighters, before darting downstairs to the living room. Warm sunlight shines in through the floor length windows, reflecting off the golden decor features in the room.

The fresh pollen scent of gerbera daisies fills my nostrils as they sit perfectly, in a white and gold vase, on the coffee table.

Bouncing onto the white couch, I pry open my books and immerse myself into the words inside. Charts and tables detailing a child's progression growing up, and how education is important for their evolution in life. Being a teacher doesn't focus on one aspect of their development, it focuses on it all. From cognitive to creative, education children correctly helps them pave their own path.

My study books are full of colorful lines as I highlight all the important parts for my curriculum. I don't even realize how submerged I am into studying that four hours have passed by me like a bird in the wind.

My dry throat forces me to take a study break to get a glass of water, but my heart drops so far into my stomach when I hear footsteps within the house. I can't pinpoint what room it's coming from because my head is pounding so hard, it throbs in my ears. My eyes dart around my surroundings so fast, it starts giving me a headache, but I try to think of an escape plan. If it's a murderer, then fine, I'll go out fighting. But if it's Stanley...I gulp.

Dread mixed with panic is a deadly cocktail that knocks all my instincts on their ass.

Like they're a sounding siren in the middle of the room, all my attention is on my stack of study books. My fingers grasp them as quickly as I can move and I shove them into the center table drawers. The only thing inside is a sewing kit, and I know Stanley won't be looking in there.

Relief floods my lungs as I take in a deep breath and dash over to the corner and pretend to clean. The fiber cloth laying on the oak table, snatching it up so quickly that the fabric catches on any dry skin on my palms.

Keeping the doorway within my eyeline, I rub circles on the oak, doing nothing other than rub dust around. I try to focus on body size, whether it's someone I know or if it's someone completely unexpected.

Loud grunts begin reverberating off the walls, and I release a breath, but it's shortly inhaled back into my lungs as anxiety increases. Saliva builds inside my mouth as my thoughts fire a mile a minute. I have a deep sense of dread in the pit of my stomach, like I've forgotten to do something, but I don't even get a free second to triple check, because a large body blocks the doorway.

Stanley's home.

"Miss me?" He grunts, limping over towards me as I pretend to act surprised at his arrival.

"Of course." I nod, begging the invisible strings attached to the corners of my mouth to lift.

I can force this marriage, but forcing my emotions is starting to become an issue. I know the repercussions if I don't make Stanley happy. I've lived that life for three years and have become a shell of myself. Terror backed me into this corner and towered over me, not allowing me to step an inch out of line without facing punishment. But terror didn't predict salvation to swoop in and show me the exit sign. A clear path lit up, guiding me towards a protector.

"Show me how much you missed me." He grunts in my ear as his large figure swallows me. His rough hands snake around my hips and he rests his chin on my shoulder, his breath wafting beer and tobacco my way.

I swallow the vomit threatening to appear. Turning my head towards him while holding my breath, I place a small peck on his lips, dry and sour.

"Come on, Elle. You missed me more than that, didn't you?" His hands trail up towards my breasts, groping them as he hums in approval.

It won't last long, I tell myself.

It'll be the same as all the other times, I tell myself.

Grasping my upper arm, he guides me towards the couch. "Show me with your mouth how much you missed your darling husband." The words are like sandpaper against teeth.

I trail behind, mentally repeating the lyrics to *Under the Bridge* by Red Hot Chilli Peppers, reassuring myself I'm okay and it isn't forever. It's become a safety net for me, reminding me this ordeal is temporary and once the lyrics are said six times, it's over.

But he stops dead in his tracks before he reaches the couch, causing me to bump into his back. "What's this?" He asks, his grit teeth barely letting the words escape.

I can't see a single thing so I try to round him, but instead, he bends in front of me, blocking my path once again. I'm desperate to see what he's referring to, panicking that Poe has accidentally gone to the toilet inside or I've spilt something on the floor. But it's much worse.

It's so much fucking worse.

"What the fuck is this?" He growls, and in his raised hand is the study book I had on my lap, separate from the rest of the pile.

Saliva feels like cotton in my throat as I try to clear the sudden lump inside of it. I can't articulate my words as my brain screams warning signs at me, activating my flight mode.

"I-" I stutter, trying to think of a good excuse, but truthfully, I'm on the verge of a full blown panic attack.

"You're studying?" His voice raised, he turns to face me, closing the gap in between us.

I back up, nausea threatening to leave my stomach. My hands shake as my adrenaline begins pumping, causing my head and heart to throb just as fast. I don't know how I'm moving right now. I'm petrified of what's about to happen, but my body is on autopilot. "I can explain." I croak, the wall behind me suddenly blocking me in.

"Explain?" He mocks my tone. "You're trying to leave me, aren't you?" Stepping away, he laughs, but there's no humor in it. He throws the book across the room, his hands shake as they clench and unclench. And just as I think he's calmed down, his palm grasps the coffee table and it flips, crashing onto the ground with broken legs.

"You can't leave me, Elle! You're my goddamn wife!" The few meters between us isn't enough space.

I nod, unable to speak with no air in my lungs, but it's not good enough for him. So he does the one thing he promised he wouldn't do again.

My vision blurs and my body snaps awake as Stanley lunges for me. His arms out in front of him, his face turns red as he bares his teeth, his eyes set on my throat.

But I don't wait for my punishment.

I bolt. My legs running so fast that my muscles should be burning, but my adrenaline saves me from pain. My vision is spotty, but I don't allow my mind to think. My escape is limited as Stanley blocks most exits, so I go to the once place I have clear access to. The bathroom.

Passing through the slim hallway, I step inside the cool room and scream for Poe. He somehow passes Stanley, and misses Stanley's wide grasp to grab him. Once Poe's inside with me, I slam the door behind me. I flick the double lock and push my palms up against the door for added weight as fat droplets begin falling from my eyes. My ears throb as my blood runs hot, every nerve inside of me on high alert. I can't slow my breathing down, the breaths burning my lungs with their rapid work.

Loud thumps sound on the other side of the door. "Open up, Elle!" Stanley roars, taking no breaks from the pounding. He jams the door handle up and down, but gets angrier when he realizes he can't come inside. "Open this fucking door, now! You're going to pay for this, you stupid slut!"

Lowering myself to the floor, I place my fingers in my ears and sing Under the Bridge, until the house falls silent.

Two painfully long hours pass, and after hearing footsteps on the floor above, I build up all the courage inside of me to unlock the door and peek into the hallway. If Stanley is upstairs, he couldn't possibly hear me tiptoe my way to the front door, and if this is the only chance I get, I'd forever hate myself if I didn't take it.

Two lefts and one right. That's all I need to take to be out of this fucking hellhole.

A light click bounces off the bathroom walls as I unlock the door, my hands wobbling with the crashed adrenaline. Slow deep breaths fill my lungs as I tell Poe to walk beside me. Slowly and lightly, we step down the hallway, the house unnervingly still without a sound inside of it.

Peering into the living room, I see the scene Stanley left. Glass shattered near the fireplace, splinters of wood scattered on the rug and slashed cushions. It's like a crime scene without the blood.

But the coast is clear, so I proceed into the kitchen. I can't hear anything, and nothing in my peripheral vision moves, so I tap my leg to encourage Poe to keep up with me as I set my sight on the front door. It's a finale, my last lap until I'm away from danger, but the last lap is always the hardest.

And I don't prepare myself for the sudden attack.

My brain has no time to even acknowledge the movement, let alone the loud howl Stanley lets out. His fists are pushed against my shoulders, forcing me against the wall with a loud thud. The force sends shockwaves up my body as my head pounds against the wall, stars blurring my vision.

"Just remember," He hisses. "You asked for this."

I don't have a chance to ask what I asked for.

Seething pain assaults my inner wrist, the scent of burnt flesh filling the air. I can't stop the scream erupting from my throat. My body's automatic response is to pull away, but Stanley's got an extreme grip on my wrist and his shoulder is forced against my throat, his body weight holding me in place.

My forearm is Stanley's next target, agony engulfing my whole arm, heat engulfing that one spot. I wail, forced to live through the pain Stanley is inflicting on me.

Yet, my cries of pain just drive him more like a deep deprived sadist, as he forces a lit cigar to my skin four more times. My vision turns obscure when the final burn meets my neck. The scent of my own burning flesh makes me retch as my skin itches for any kind of relief.

The lyrics don't work this time.

Torture forces my screams to sound louder than the words in my mind.

I was stupid enough to believe promises are to be kept. Especially by a man who used dirty authority to get his own way.

Like jelly, my legs can't hold the weight of my damaged body any longer. Relying solely on Stanley to hold me up, he pulls his weight off of me and I crash to the ground like a weight off a building.

I don't watch where he goes. My mind is a cloud of misery; I don't have the mental capacity to acknowledge anything, other than my own wrongdoings. I brought this upon myself, and I couldn't hate myself anymore than I do right now.

But it's not just about me.

Poe.

Objects are foggy, but I can make out outlines. The kitchen table, the cabinets, the refrigerator. The big ball of fluff, cowering under the table.

My heart aches, knowing my baby is so full of fear that he has to try and hide. He doesn't cower unless he's been punished. Thanks to Stanley's unknown hatred towards Poe, I figured out Poe's fear towards Stanley when he would try to discipline him for being a normal energetic puppy.

My mind wasn't sharp enough to witness what Stanley did to him this time, but I'm not wasting another minute allowing Poe to shake in terror. Whether Stanley comes for me or not, giving Poe an escape route is my sole focus.

Every inch of my body is in anguish, but I muster all my strength and push my palms into the ground. Tucking my feet under my thighs, I push myself upwards and rise to my feet. I can't rely on my sight or hearing right now, considering they're still feeling the effects of Stanley's punishment. Having no valuable instincts to run off of, I do the only thing I can in this situation.

"Poe." My voice is a grating whisper, but it gains his attention. "Come on, boy." The instruction is soft, but he seems to pick up on the urgency in my voice. With a glance around the room, Poe rises to his feet and walks over to me. He nuzzles his head beside my thigh, a sign of protection, and looks up at me.

My tear covered eyes look down at him as I inhale a deep breath. "Run." I command, my voice shaking as my adrenaline begins pumping through my veins once again.

The command was for Poe, but I follow my own guidance. My sight is set on the front door, with sun shining in through the panes of glass, it's easy to spot. Like a woosh of energy has shot through me, I begin sprinting towards the door, Poe hot on my heels. Each step feels like a knife in the foot, each injured part of my body taking in turns to spasm in pain. But I don't slow down.

We don't slow our steps once we are out the door.

We don't slow our steps when we pass the seafront.

And we don't slow our steps when we run through town.

We only come to a grinding halt once we reach Aspen Avenue.

Our only chance to seek refuge and rescue.

13

JOHNNY

Unnervingly loud thumping sounds on the other side of my door, making the vibrations reach me in the shower. Flicking the hot water off, I grab a towel and wrap it around my waist, fastening it in place. The thumps echo again, urging me to hurry up and make my way to the door. Leaving a trail of wet foot marks along the laminate floor, I turn around to go and dry my feet, but I quickly ignore the mess I'm making the third time my door gets hit.

I don't hear anything on the other side, instantly raising my guard. My gaze darts to my gun on the table, mentally calculating how far away it is in case I need to use it. I'm not dressed for a fight, my dignity would reach zero if I had to defend myself. I don't even have time to grab my phone to check my door camera.

My fist clutches the door knob and I twist, mentally preparing myself for anything when opening, but as the cool draft brushes my face, my heart sinks so low in my stomach, it aches.

Tear stained cheeks, dark circles under her eyes and burn marks up her arm, Elle stands on the other side, her shoulders slumped and lip wobbling. "Fuck, baby. Come here." I push the door wider and open my arms. Her stiff body melts into mine as she begins sobbing, defeated noises escaping her lips as she gasps for air. "I'm going to kill him." The words escape my lips as if they're spiked with venom.

"No." Elle's plea is instant, and against every fighting nerve inside of my body, I decide against my own wishes and do as Elle says. "Please don't leave me."

The lump in my throat forces me to swallow as the weight in my chest feels almost too heavy to breathe. I swear I can hear my heart crack after seeing Elle in such a fragile, damaged state.

I guide Elle towards the couch and encourage her to sit. She looks numb. A vacant gaze in her eyes and her breathing labored, she's detached herself from her feelings as her adrenaline wears off from whatever the fuck Stanley did to her.

Grabbing a blanket from the couch corner, I place it over her legs and tap the cushion next to her for Poe to jump up. If anyone can comfort her in this moment of vulnerability, it's Poe. Crouching in front of Elle, I place my hands on top of her interlocked ones and meet her eyes. I feel sick from the agony in her sunken eyes. "I'm going to get dressed then I'll be right back, okay Violet?"

If I wasn't so close to her, I wouldn't have seen her nod.

Making sure I don't leave Elle alone for any longer than I need to, I quickly chuck on some joggers and a t-shirt. I double check the door is locked on my way through to the living room, before pulling the foot stool over to sit in front of Elle.

It's breaking my heart just looking at her, yet the anger low in my stomach isn't allowing me to forget it's there. I want to do to Stanley what he did to Elle, and then torture him some more. Show him what it's like to use power against someone who's defenseless.

I don't realize how hard I'm gritting my teeth until pain shoots along my jaw, pulling me back to the present. I fucking hate this. I hate that I need to ask what he did when she's already mentally crushed. But I can't help if I'm in the dark.

"Elle," my hands grasp her ice cold ones, her gaze still empty. "I'm sorry I have to ask." My words are lodged in my throat. "What did he do to you?"

Her eyes are glass, each emotion she's feeling is shattering inside of her. Glazed eyes finally meet mine, an agonizing sob escaping her lips as she grips my hands tight.

I can barely watch without wanting to put my fist through a fucking wall. Wrapping my arm around her back, I pull her close to my chest, desperate to take away every ounce of torment she's being drowned by. My t-shirt begins dampening as Elle bawls her eyes out, her fists grasping onto the thin fabric.

I don't interfere. I let her cry and wail as she nuzzles her head into my neck. She can use me as a punching bag, a release, an outlet for her suffering.

Give me all your pain, Elle.

"I'm sorry," the croak that escapes Elle's lips catches me by surprise as she slowly leans backwards, grasping my warm hands into her cold ones.

"You have nothing to be sorry for, Violet." The reassurance falls flat as she opens her mouth to apologize again. "Elle. Don't apologize. You can trust me, remember?"

I swear I see the smallest smile lift on her lips, the gesture warming my heart. Her gaze looks around the room as her mouth falls open and shuts at least three times before any sound comes out. Her eyes are glued to our connected hands, but she doesn't pull away, and I don't force her to look at me, either. "He caught me studying." She snuffles, her voice soft. "I tried to apologize but he was still drunk from wherever he was last night."

The Boathouse Diner.

With me.

Shit.

"Me and Poe locked ourselves in the bathroom for hours. I thought the coast was clear, so we ran, but he caught me before I could make it out the front door." Tears begin falling from her lost eyes, but she powers on, her voice wobbling. "He burnt me." Elle's left arm is extended, small circular marks of burnt skin dotted up her arm. She turns her head to the side slightly, and I spot one on her neck. The deep red skin is slightly raised, the area around the burn a lighter red color.

Rage blurs my vision the longer I look at her wounds. I'm not a violent person; I'm a levelheaded investigator who can do a job professionally and respectfully. Yet, right now, I'm anything but. Murderous thoughts contaminate my mind with visions of what I could do to Stanley. Cut off his individual fingers, slice his achilles heel, feed him his own tongue. Each one is more tempting than the last.

But I can't jeopardize anything else happening to Elle. She's never returning to that house while that repulsive son of a bitch is inside of it.

A sigh escapes my lips as I build up the confidence to tell her I need to document her injuries for the case. I feel sick at the thought of her feeling objectified. "I want him dead for what he's done to you, Violet, but to put him away forever, I need to collect evidence to use against him." I try to explain as gently as possible, the pads of my thumbs circling her soft hands. Her doe eyes watch me, her eyebrows pulled together as if she doesn't follow what I'm saying. "I need to take photos of your burns. But we can take as much time as you need. If you need a break, just tell me, and I'll stop."

She takes a moment of deliberation before gently nodding, gulping back her anxiety.

My thumb finds her cheek as I swipe away a stray tear, my stomach in knots witnessing her anguish. "I'm really sorry this happened to you, Elle."

A humorless smile tugs at her lips and a single nod.

I rise to my feet and grab my phone from the table, flicking the camera on. "Remember, we can stop if you want to. I'll be as quick as I can." Grasping her left hand gently, I hold it upwards, turning it slightly so I have a clear view of the burns. Elle's gaze is focused in the opposite direction out the window, her free hand held tightly between her knees as her legs bounce. I can see the fast rise and fall of her chest and the anxious way she's nibbling on her bottom lip, but I don't want to do anything that will agitate her. I'm already pushing her personal space by taking these photos, I'm not pushing my luck any further.

A few wide shots and an individual up close photo of each burn, I quickly lock my phone and throw it onto the couch, away from Elle. I gently place her hand back down on her lap and I begin lowering myself back down onto the foot stool, but Elle's soft voice pauses my movements.

"Please just hold me." Her plea is more than enough for me to plop myself on the couch next to her, my arm around her back as her head rests on my shoulder. Silence engulfs us, the only sound I can hear is our in sync breathing.

I want to erase every single negative thing she's ever experienced. Every worry, every pain, every goddamn burn she had to endure. The pain I feel for this woman isn't something I'd wish on my worst enemy. But feeling her close to my body eases the dull ache in my gut. She feels like that moment of reflection where life couldn't get any better. The memory your mind always goes back to when you think of a moment you were truly happy. Elle Adams is the definition of being on top of the world.

A raspy cough slips from Elle's mouth and it occurs to me she's been in a sea of tears, her throat probably feels like sandpaper. "Do you want a glass of water?" I'm up and heading towards the kitchen before she gives me a response. "Here," I pass Elle the full glass, taking a seat next to her.

Taking slow sips, she eventually finishes the water but keeps ahold of the glass, tapping it while she stares into the distance. After a few seconds, her voice sounds somewhat hydrated. "Does it make me a bad person to want him to spend the rest of his life in jail?" Her voice is quiet, but I can hear the emotion drowning her. She actually thinks she'd be a bad person for wanting her abuser to rot in a cell. I must be unforgivable for wanting him six feet under.

"You could never be a bad person, Elle. Jail is too kind a punishment for a man like him." Without thinking, I place a kiss on her forehead. The sudden shock hits me like a stack of bricks. I shouldn't have done that. She's vulnerable and in shock, and I've just invaded her personal space.

But her ocean blue eyes meet mine, warmth pooling inside of them. The six-inch gap between our lips becomes five as Elle edges forward. Five becomes four, and before I know it, her sweet lips are placed onto mine.

Like our first kiss, it's slow. Soaking in every second I'm connected to this woman, I inhale her scent and memorize the taste of her lips. My hand finds its way to her heated cheek, her skin like silk under my touch. Passion builds a perfect empire between us as our kiss deepens. She invites my tongue inside her hot mouth, her arm around my waist as she lays backwards. I'm on top of her, my body flush against hers. I can feel the swell of her pert breasts, her delicate hips and the dip in her waist. My hips grind downwards, but the movement sends a shock through my body.

"Elle." My voice comes out a rasp as I pull my lips from hers. "You're vulnerable and not in the right headspace right now." I want to fucking punch myself for ruining a moment like this, but it's not about me. It's about Elle and doing what's right for her.

I can see the disappointment in her eyes. "For once in my life, I'm in control. My headspace is perfectly clear." Her eyes fall to my lips, but they bounce back up to my eyes when I don't close the gap.

"If you really mean that, we can revisit this once you've slept on it." I place a kiss on her forehead just so I don't have to look at the defeat in her eyes.

"Always a gentleman." She rolls her eyes, the corners of her lips lifting.

I can't stop the smile from taking over my face. "Come here," I lift her off the couch and sit down in her spot, turning her body so she's laying on top of me. Her head on my chest, I rub my hand through her velvet hair, smelling her rose scented shampoo. I comfort her until she falls asleep, and with her light breaths sounding below me, I fall out of consciousness, too.

I'd do anything for the woman who has her hands wrapped around my heart so tightly. Including ruining her bastard husband.

14

ELLE

A heavy weight is draped over my waist as my body awakens from its deep sleep. Instant panic forces my eyes wide open as my mind tells me it's Stanley asleep behind me, but the room isn't my own. Oak floors with black walls, the bed is placed in the center of the room, with a chair propped in the corner and a black wooden bedside table. I turn my body onto my back so I can get a good look at my surroundings. Floor to ceiling windows with floor length blackout curtains, a gray footstool in the corner and a gorgeous abstract art print on the wall in front of the bed.

Glancing to my left, I take in Johnny's sleeping appearance. His mouth slightly agape as he breathes slowly and evenly. He looks so peaceful as his cheek rests on my shoulder. His short stubble itches my bare skin, and I notice I'm still in my dress from yesterday. I was so exhausted after yesterday's events that I don't remember anything after falling asleep on the couch.

Shit. Poe is probably starving. I didn't even feed him last night. Lightly grasping Johnny's warm arm, I slowly lift him off me and shuffle out of bed. Padding my feet across the cool floor, I close the door behind me and go on a search for Poe around Johnny's apartment. Whisper shouting Poe's name, I don't hear his little paws tapping along the floor. Checking each room, I can't find him anywhere. Panic sets in as self blame smacks me in the face. I should have kept an eye on him yesterday.

A deep breath fills my lungs as I try to calm myself and think with a clear mind. Except, my brain is all fog. Fog from what I endured yesterday, fog at what happened last night, and more thick fog as I think about the future.

The thought makes me feel sick.

Shaking my head, I try to focus on now. I need to find my bundle of fluff before I lose my mind. My feet get used to the cold floor, but I'm not looking where I'm going and my foot lands on something hard and loud. The ceramic sound sends shockwaves through me and I jump out of my skin, my hand on my chest to feel something solid.

An empty bowl on the floor next to the breakfast bar, now spinning slowly after I stepped on it. Next to it is a bowl full of water.

I gulp as my heart swells.

Johnny took care of Poe while I was asleep.

He fed him and made sure he had something to drink.

Oh my god.

I can't stop the tears from brimming my lash line.

Stanley hates Poe, yet Johnny takes care of him.

"Hey." Johnny's voice croaks as he peers around the corner, his eyes still tired and his hair disheveled. "You okay? What's up?" He closes the gap between us and holds me, allowing me to inhale his scent to ground myself.

"I can't find Poe." I say, my voice wobbling as I try to hold back the flood of emotions prying their way through.

"He's asleep next to the bed." Johnny rubs the back of my head, each stroke taking a pound of weight off my shoulders.

The sigh of relief that escapes my lips makes my shoulders drop, finally allowing myself a slow, calm breath.

I'm a ball of anxiety and I need something to bring my stress levels down. "Can I have a shower?"

"Of course you can." Johnny pulls himself back slightly so he can look at me. His hands on my cheeks, his eyes gaze at me, studying my expression. "You don't have to ask, Violet. Whatever you want, I'll make it happen."

His kindness feels foreign. I hate that my mind automatically goes to Johnny wanting something from me to use against me. I'm used to insults and tension. Not compassion and generosity. The feeling that this is too good to be true is suffocating me.

"I'll grab you a t-shirt to wear afterwards. Take your time. I'll be out here if you need me." He must catch my eyes as they peep at the room where Poe is in. "I'll feed him and take him out."

My words are stuck in my throat. All I can muster is a pathetic nod before excusing myself.

The bathroom is lit up with warm lighting, a large walk in shower to the right and a porcelain bathtub to the left. I lock the door behind me and begin undressing, letting my clothes pool beneath me. My skin instantly breaks out in goosebumps as the cool air hits my bare body, but I welcome the feeling. I'm not here to take a hot shower. I want an ice cold one. I need my puffy eyes to look less puffy, and my burns to feel soothed.

I need that refreshed feeling where my body feels awake and ready for the day.

Flicking the tap to cold, streams of water gush down to the tiled floor. I take a breath of preparation before stepping under the constant flow of water, my body instantly awakening. My first instinct is to run towards a towel, but I don't give in. The goosebumps slowly fade away and my body reels itself back in from the shock of coldness. Once adjusted, I thrive under the low temperature.

Grabbing the body wash on the shelf, I pop the lid and squeeze a dollop into my hand. The scent invades my nostrils immediately. Mandarin and spice forms a blanket of safety around me, reassuring me more than Stanley ever could.

Lathering it in my hands, I wash myself, avoiding my wounds, before turning the shower off. I grab the gray towel on the radiator and wrap it around my body, the soft fabric instantly warming my skin. I swipe the steam from the mirror, small droplets sliding downwards and dripping into the sink. Catching my own reflection, I stare at the woman who gazes back at me and I tell her she's worth so much more than what Stanley has put her through.

Like Johnny said, he's laid out a t-shirt on the bed for me to wear. It's black, soft, and it's *him*. I dry myself and put the t-shirt on, towel drying my hair enough for it to stop dripping.

Hanging the towel up to dry, I sit on the edge of the bed and wait for Johnny and Poe to return. I sit like my only purpose is to guard the bed. There's not much in Johnny's apartment to entertain me and I don't want to go through his personal things.

I don't want to impose, but I feel safe with Johnny. I've gotten so used to my own isolation that I forgot how *good* it felt to have good company. I always thought isolation was better than bad company, I didn't even consider how much better my life could be if someone who actually cared about me came along. I'm used to living on the edge of a cliff, constantly fearing leaning too far. But it's not like that with Johnny. It feels smooth and slow, like I have both hands on the wheel, directing my own life.

"We're back!" Johnny's voice bellows from the front door, and in a few seconds, Poe comes into the bedroom and greets me. He's full of energy as he bounces up onto the bed.

Gasping, I try to encourage him down from the bed, panic setting in at Poe already pushing limits.

"He's fine," Johnny waves me off. "Nice shirt by the way."

"Thanks." I smile, rising to my feet. "Some guy let me wear it while I take over his apartment." I wave my hand around and roll my eyes jokingly.

"I bet he's glad you're here." He reaches past me to place Poe's lead onto the bedside table, his chest brushing along my clothed nipple.

Instant butterflies swarm my stomach at the sensitive touch, awakening that temptation inside of me I forgot I had. He stands back to his full height, but I can't focus on anything other than how close he is to me. Heat radiates from his body as he peers down at me, his eyes fixed on mine.

Last night is a memory that sits at the front of my mind. His lips against mine, his hands in my hair. How *good* it felt to have him on top of me.

I want to feel that good again.

"My headspace is clear." The words are a whisper from my lips, but they're laced with desire.

His eyes squint slightly, but recognition hits him a few seconds after. He closes the gap between us, his hands on my hips, his lips mere centimeters from mine. "Are you sure?"

The temperature in the room has suddenly increased, my skin sensitive and wanting. "I'm sure." I nod, the anticipation thick between us.

But Johnny doesn't waste a second longer. Like time is of the essence, his lips crash against mine, taking all I can give. My hands loop around the back of his neck, his hands on my thighs as he hoists me up around his waist. The bulge in his joggers is already hard, igniting my desire deep to my core.

He holds me at the end of the bed before gently placing me down below him. Our mouths are locked together like our lives depend on it. His tongue inside my mouth sends heat to my core, lighting a fire inside of me at the thought of his tongue on my pussy.

Johnny's teeth pull my bottom lip into his mouth as he gently nibbles and sucks, the erotic feeling pulling a moan from my lips. My hands find the bottom of his shirt and I yank it over his head and discard it to the side.

My mouth nearly falls agape at the sight of him. Like he was crafted by god himself, his toned abs carved perfectly, his skin tanned, and his left arm decorated with a tattooed sleeve. I knew he was all muscle, but I didn't think he was hiding all of this under those thin t-shirts.

His knee nudges my legs open, and I comply without a second thought. Spreading my legs, Johnny leans forward, his lips never leaving my own. My pussy dampens as I realize the only thing separating us right now is his joggers. One thin piece of fabric stopping me from giving into the dirty thoughts that have plagued my mind for the past couple months.

Grabbing my t-shirt at the hem, he gently pulls it over my head, exposing my naked body. Paranoia takes over and I try to pull him down so I'm covered, including the burns on my arm, but he's too strong to move. He hovers above me, his eyes trailing down my body painfully slow, like he's trying to memorize every inch of me. "So fucking perfect." He growls, his tongue swiping along his bottom lip.

He begins shaking his head, instantly making my eyes widen that he's about to pick out an insecurity. He picks up on my expression and places a soft kiss between my breasts. "I can't believe you're real, Violet. Every goddamn inch of you doesn't have a single fault."

I can't stop the whimper escaping my lips. My body feels electric, and every time Johnny touches me, a jolt of power floods through me. He's valuing every inch of me, making me feel I'm the best thing he's ever laid eyes on.

I've never felt so wanted in my life.

His hot mouth is around my pebbled nipple, sucking and flicking, while his hand lightly pinches my other. A groan vibrates from Johnny's lips, sending waves of pleasure straight to my pussy. I'm dripping with need, desperate to feel him between my legs. Trailing wet kisses down my stomach, each one longer than the last. His eyes peer up at me as he reaches my clit and I watch his tongue as it glides along my pussy.

My back arches at the heat between my legs, my orgasm already threatening to appear. He laps and sucks my clit, each stroke a perfect pace for heat to coil in my lower belly. My hand finds its way into Johnny's hair as I tug and thrust into his face. Each nerve ending inside of me is sparking with pleasure, forcing my vision to blur and my muscles to contract.

He places one finger inside of me, curling it to hit that spot as he thrusts in and out. Adding a second finger, he groans as I moan his name, finger fucking me at a constant pace. My legs spread with his face between them, the image alone is enough to send me over the edge.

Stars blur my vision and my ears throb as my body feels like it's weightless. My pussy convulses as Johnny fingers and licks me through my orgasm, his eyes pinned on me as I shamelessly whimper. Toes curling and fists gripping anything I can get my hands on, I try to ground myself, but I'm so high on pleasure that my sense of surroundings are nonexistent.

I feel the loss immediately as Johnny withdraws his fingers, but I'm instantly turned on after watching him place those exact fingers that were just inside of me, inside of his mouth.

"You taste so fucking good." He groans, lowering his mouth to my pussy again and licking up every ounce of my come. That sight alone is enough to tempt me with another pending orgasm.

He rises to his full height, and his erection is obvious through his joggers. With one quick pull, his joggers pool on the floor with the rest of his clothes, his cock thick, ready and dripping in precum.

My eyes widen at the sheer size of him, mentally questioning how the fuck that's supposed to fit inside of me. "It's okay, Violet." Johnny coo's, leaning over me. "We'll take it slow."

His skin feels like silk against mine. Hot and soft, his hands lightly swipe down my cheek before placing a kiss against my lips. He's gentle and sweet, but the man who was just between my legs was anything but. I know why he's being gentle with me, but I want to leave that life and anything that relates to it in the past. I'm not damaged unless I make that my story.

"I'm not a broken doll, Johnny. You don't need to hold back." I assure him, his eyes fixed on mine for a few seconds before nodding for confirmation.

His hands find my hips as he places his mouth over mine, teasing me with his tip. But I can see the desperation in his eyes, and it doesn't take him long to give in. With one thrust, he pushes his full length inside of me, both pulling a gasp out of our mouths. Us both being in sync is erotic, like we cause the same effect on each other.

My body takes a minute to adjust to his size, but slowly, Johnny begins thrusting back and forth, each stroke more dominant than the last. One of his hands in my hair and the other on my hip to help him thrust, Johnny fucks me fiercely and passionately like this is the only chance he'll ever get.

Moans and sweat fill the air as Johnny pulls me up so I'm slouched on the pillows, him leaning over the top of me. Our lips graze each others, stealing kisses every chance we get. "You're so beautiful, Elle." Johnny pants. I assume he means my body when having sex like most guys think about, but his eyes are glued to mine, desire swimming within his irises. "So fucking beautiful."

My emotions are on overdrive right now, and his compliment sunk deeper than I care to admit. A part of me feels guilty for sleeping with Johnny while I'm married, but most of me feels a sense of empowerment for doing something I want to do. I want to give all my time to this man because he makes me feel so fucking good. I feel seen, admired and beautiful. He's the kind of man to protect with his whole heart and pick a single girl out in a crowd because he only has eyes for her.

I want to be that girl.

Lewd sounds echo around the room as Johnny's thrusts get erratic. Each moan and whimper getting louder the longer we fuck. That familiar feeling begins brimming as my orgasm threatens to erupt, my sense of reality beginning to fade. But I don't have much warning this time as my orgasm peaks.

"Fuck, come with me, baby. You're taking me so fucking well."

I don't need to be told again. I'm in a bubble floating on a cloud of euphoria as my pussy clenches around Johnny's cock, thrusting us through our pleasure like we're synced. I grasp and scratch his back as I moan his name over and over, his mouth over mine as he drinks my words up. I can't see, my eyes speckled with spots as my body feels weightless. Stray strands of my hair stick to my glazed forehead, but my appearance is the least of my concerns right now. I'm too focused on how fucking good I feel.

That's what passionate sex feels like.

And it's addictive.

As Johnny slows his thrusts, he swipes my stray hairs out of my face, his eyes fixed on mine. He doesn't say anything, instead, he places a delicate kiss on my lips. "You're one of a kind, Elle Adams." That gorgeous smile lifts his cheeks, never breaking eye contact.

"That's my married name." I correct him, although I'm not sure why. Maybe it's because I hate every link I have to Stanley.

"My bad." He doesn't ask for my maiden name. Instead he smirks at me. I'm confused why, but his mouth falls open as he talks again. "You're one of a kind, Elle Darby. It's a once in a lifetime chance our paths crossed. I'll spend the rest of my life being grateful that I'm blessed with your existence."

I'm about to question how he knows my maiden name to distract myself from the emotion welling in my throat, but it hits me that he's a personal investigator. Of course he knows my name.

"I'm so glad I met you." I wasn't sure if the words would even escape my mouth, but they come out as a whisper.

The silence that gathers around us is comfortable and reassuring. I don't feel on edge or unsafe. It's unusual, but I like it.

Johnny sighs deeply before pulling out of me and grabbing a towel. He cleans me before pulling the duvet over me and sliding underneath, pulling me onto his chest. "Please don't return to him."

My eyes dart upwards to his, but I don't know what to say. I don't want to return to Stanley, ever. It's not even something

I'm considering, but he owns my life. I'm still his wife and it's not like I have enough of my own money to up and leave him.

"A lot of compelling evidence is currently being reviewed to use against Stanley, the rest of the council and police department. You can stay here until he's taken care of." I nod vacantly at the realization of how real this is. I don't even know how to process it in my brain. I have feelings for the man who's taking down my husband.

Shit.

My subconscious admitted it without asking my brain first, but I can't deny it. While the past couple months have been a whirlwind, Johnny is the person I think of first thing in the morning and the last thing at night. I didn't think my heart would allow itself to open up to someone ever again, but Johnny took me by surprise. He didn't give me reason to overthink and evaluate everything he does. He gave me time and space to process, a shoulder to cry on and a protector in my corner.

If this is a taste of what the future can offer, then I want to experience it with Johnny by my side.

I don't know what's happening between us and I don't need to know right now. I just need things to stay the way they are, in this bubble of safety, until the current settles and I can breathe again.

15

JOHNNY

I would say I have limits, but apparently they aren't present when a married woman is my sole interest. At first, I thought it was a fascination, but fascinations don't clench my heart the way she does.

I keep peeling off her layers and watching her true self become more visible with each peel. It's beautiful to see Elle become who she truly is, instead of being forced to be someone she's not. It fills me with joy to know she feels safe enough with me to be herself and not fear acting a certain way will get her punished.

She's spent the past few days at my apartment, where she can feel safe and I can keep an eye on her to make sure Stanley isn't within assaulting distance. I've given her full access to my laptop so she can study and I dropped her off at a small clothes store to get some clothes so she doesn't need to wear my t-shirts anymore. I'm devastated, because she looks goddamn perfect dressed in my clothes and nothing underneath.

I've had a few days break from work while the evidence against Charlestown's men in power I collected is analyzed and used to build a case. Telling my workplace I need a few personal days off, I've been focusing all my attention on Elle. Late mornings, staying awake all night while I'm buried deep inside of her, learning every curve and dip on her delicate body.

I didn't know there was something deeper than sex. I've never had the opportunity to experience that because I had no interest in it. Yet, here I am, immersed in a world where sex means so much more than physical attraction. The feeling inside of me that tells me Elle's needs come before my own screams louder than the desire to finish myself off. It's understanding each other's souls and what each other needs in a moment of intimacy. I like feeling vulnerable when it's Elle looking at me.

I don't want to push her boundaries and I don't want to scare her so I'll keep my internal thoughts to myself. This thing between us is no longer a neighbor in passing or a colleague of her husbands. My heart beats for Elle Darby, and if it takes the rest of my life proving to her how extraordinary she is, then I better live a long goddamn life.

Leaning against my door frame, I stand mesmerized as I gaze at Elle, who's sleeping peacefully with her mouth slightly agape, her breathing slow and steady. I can't pull my eyes away from her adorable button nose and her perfect pink cheeks. Like a sleeping angel, I take a mental picture of her and soak in this moment where she looks truly relaxed.

The loud buzzing from my phone in the living room catches my attention, and I jog in the room quickly to answer it so it doesn't wake Elle. "Miller." I answer, leaning the back of my thighs against the table.

"We've nearly finished reviewing the footage." My data analyst tells me in a gruff voice. I'm sure he's been lacking sleep combing through the heap of evidence I collected. Catching this drug operation is the agency's most important case right now, since I made them aware of other civilians getting harmed in the process. "A location was mentioned for the drop. It's registered to three people."

"Who?" I press.

"Clyde Beasley, Peter Beasley and Stanley Adams."

"Where?" I answer abruptly, putting him on loud speaker and loading up maps on my phone.

"Dusty Road Warehouse."

I search the location on maps, but the only place that pops up is a road called Dusty Road. I put it onto satellite view, and I see a single warehouse surrounded by sealed off construction that looks completely abandoned.

"There's more," my analyst says, his tone optimistic. "There's a papertrail of money transfers linking to each member we suspected to be a part of the trade. All cash transactions going in and out with the reference set as Dusty Road. The warehouse was purchased four years ago and since then, their business has been increasing. We'll need a little more time to track down their buyers and who they get their merchandise from, but we have enough to put Charlestown's criminals away for life."

Relief settles in my stomach. "I'll take a look and scope out the area and wait for the crime squad to arrive. I'm tagging in." I confirm, before hanging up and grabbing my keys and gun. I want to be there to see the look on Stanley's face when betrayal stings him. I'll slap the handcuffs on a little too hard and use lethal force if need be to drown him in fear, just so he feels that twinge of panic that he might not make it out of today alive. Just like he did with Elle.

Quickly scribbling on a note to let Elle know where I am if she wakes up, I double check my front door camera is on, in case any unwanted visitors show up, before sneaking out the front door.

Hopping into my Land Rover, I force the stick into drive and follow the map directions. Everything in Charlestown looks normal, like a perfect small town, but this place is anything but. Abusive councilors, drug operations, the people trusted the most are the ones who would risk your life instead of theirs.

I pass the city hall building on my way, my fists clenching at the thought of Stanley being the other side of the brick wall. My skin buzzes knowing I could show him what it feels like to be defenseless, but I can't ruin this. The agency is depending on me. Elle's depending on me. I can't fuck it up.

I'm glad Mayor Clyde didn't question my request for personal leave the night Elle came knocking at my door. He gave his permission and I thanked him, not realizing his right hand man's wife would be the reason I don't want to fucking return to that toxic place. How fucking stupid does a man need to be to not realize this is a set up? I'm not attending work the week of their big drug drop off. Sirens should be blaring in Mayor Clyde's mind, but he thinks he's untouchable, complacency is the biggest downfall of idiots like them.

I'll show him how untouchable he really is when he's looking down the barrel of my gun. They trusted the wrong person. They'll have plenty of time to reflect on their mistakes while they're rotting away in a jail cell.

Karma always bites back.

Hard enough to leave a permanent mark.

I park my car in the local tool shop car park and walk half a mile towards the location. It's the end of a neighborhood road, and it looks somewhat out of place. A silver wire gate is blocking a single road with six warning signs attached. Scaffolding inside the gate is a perfect cover, chains keep two gates fixed together with no other access points into the warehouse road. I shoot my boss a quick text, informing him of the situation.

No access points off the neighborhood road. Will need to find another way in.

Sliding my phone back into my pocket, I check my surroundings to make sure they're clear before grasping the top of the gate. I pull myself up, my muscles contracting as they hold my body weight, before swinging my legs around and jumping down the opposite side.

Dust attacks the fresh air around me as the ground changes in an instant. On the other side of the gate is tarmac road and stoned pavements. On this side of the gate, it's dust and grit along an off road strip. I see why they call it Dusty Road.

My phone buzzes in my pocket and I quickly pull it out, making sure it's not Elle in need of something, but it's just my boss.

Found a back entrance in the fields. ETA 5 minutes.

With my right hand resting on my gun, my eyes pick out any sign of movement in the distance. I'm not expecting Mayor Beasley and his bitches to be here already, considering we are an hour out of their agreed time, but he could have watchers. There's thousands of dollars worth of drugs in that warehouse, he'd be stupid to leave it unoccupied.

Maintaining my cover, I move towards a door on the side of the building. With my gun raised, I stop and listen but it's deathly silent. Testing the handle, making more noise than I'd like, the door swings open to reveal a large open area filled with hay bales being used as tables but it's what is on the bales that interests me.

I place my gun back into my holster and head over to one of the hundred stacks of packages and pick one up. It's light but compact and filled with whatever is inside of it. The duct tape exterior looks familiar to the other drug cases I've been on, but I want to be sure, so I pull out my pocket knife and make a small slice in one.

White powder, as expected.

Those fucking scumbags.

Grasping my phone from my pocket, I text my boss.

I'm inside. No one is at the location. They have a fuck tonne of drugs in here.

I watch the text bubbles pop up.

Fucking knew it. We're suiting up for the breach. Come get your gear on.

I slide my phone back into my pocket and exit the building through a different rusted door this time, making my way over to my real team. .

It's a waiting game now, and that happens to be one of my favorites.

Sitting in my boss's Mercedes, I strap up my bulletproof vest and place my earpiece in my ear. *Back in Black* by AC/DC thrums quietly on the radio as I pop my magazine out from my gun to check my clip is full for the tenth time. Grabbing another magazine, I slide it into my back pocket, just in case it turns into a shoot out.

The minutes pass by painfully slow, each second ticking longer than the last. But then my mind drifts off to Elle and I'm filled with a need to end this shitshow of an operation. She'll be free from Stanley after tonight and she can begin living her life again.

Buzzing sounds from my pocket, grabbing my attention, but as I'm about to grab my phone, multiple headlights gleam in the distance next to the warehouse, one after the other. I snag the binoculars from the dash and hold them up to my eyes. Mayor Clyde's car, Sheriff Beasley's car, and a few others park next to each other outside the location, before more people pile out of the vehicles. I don't need to sit and study each person because I know who they are. Instead, I send the go signal through the earpiece and get out of the car. I check my phone before we begin the breach to check the notification, but my eyebrows instantly drop at the sight of my camera sensor app. It detected movement, so I click on it to investigate. No one is entering my apartment, but rather leaving; Elle and Poe are on their way out somewhere. Uncertainty fills me with not knowing where she's off to. She hasn't texted me and she knows her safety isn't protected right now. But I'm not home to help her with whatever reason she's leaving the apartment.

I gather myself and take a deep breath, reassuring myself Stanley can't hurt her when he's inside the warehouse. She's not walking into danger because her abuser is about to be faced with me. I need my head in the game right now, for Elle's safety and my own. I can't protect her if I'm dead.

Drug squad agents begin treading lightly, dressed in full gear, with guns raised towards the warehouse. If you didn't know they were here, you would never know, because they're so quiet, even their vibrations they let off from each step is near enough non-existent. We move in formation as one, each person knowing their target and goal.

Anticipation builds inside of me like a drug fix, which is ironic considering the situation I'm currently in.

As we reach the location, we split off to our target areas. Waiting for the countdown, my partner crouches by our breach door while I stand, guns raised. Each door is covered by agents preparing for an immediate breach and arrest. Blood pumps in my ears as the adrenaline gives me tunnel vision. I'm solely focused on my targets with my only intent to disarm them and force them to comply.

3.

2.

1.

"Go! Go! Go!" comes through our earpieces and we move as one.

My foot slams into the wooden door, forcing it open and breaking off its hinges. Although there is only natural light filtering in through the windows, I can see easily enough, making out the figures standing around the hay bales. Commands and directions are shouted in low, dominant voices for targets to get on the floor, guns and lasers pointed at their heads and chests. My voice is a growl as I'm driven to put these men on the ground, face down where I step. Screams of protest are bouncing off the walls, pleads of apologies and blames aimed at their other men. But they comply. Laying face down on the floor, hands behind their heads and their mouths shut, officers begin making arrests.

I catch a glance of Mayor Clyde to my left with a foot placed on his back, and I yank my cuffs out from my back pocket. My feet thump with each step, my lips tight in a line as my anger boils inside of me.

I can see the moment he recognizes me as his eyes widen and his mouth falls open while he tries to lift his head off the floor. "Johnny?" He questions in disbelief, his breathing getting heavier as his body rises and falls.

"Surprise. Bet you didn't see that coming, did you?" I taunt him, placing my knee on his back as I bend to arrest him. I twist the cuffs onto his wrists, tightening them enough to pinch his skin.

He hisses in pain, trying to wiggle free from the heavy duty metal. "What?" He shakes his head, breathless and in shock. "You did this?" His tone sounds traitorous, like I'm the worst person he's ever known. He needs to take a better look at his friends before worrying about me.

I nod, unable to contain the smirk on my face. "It's Detective, not Johnny." I correct him, my tone laced with venom this time. "Now, tell me where Stanley is."

His face contorts at my question so I press my knee further into his back, making him yelp in protest. "Stanley isn't here. He didn't come to work today. Something about him and his wife so he's taking personal time off."

Loud thrums sound in my ears as my stomach sinks, panic clawing its way up my throat. I can't focus because my heart is pumping so hard it hurts.

His words repeat in my head. *Stanley's not here.*
Fuck.

This can't be fucking happening.

If Stanley isn't here, and Elle left my apartment, there's no one to keep her safe from the man who has nothing to lose. He'll do whatever he can to keep his toy by his side.

She's a mouse walking into a snake's death trap with no protection.

And this snake happens to be a fucking sadist.

16

ELLE

Sandpaper is softer than my throat right now as I gaze at the exterior of my home. A bittersweet image staring back at me, this home has been my residence for the past three years, yet it's where all my nightmares came true. I don't feel safe here, but it's the only solitude I had since my mother died.

That was, until Johnny came along.

While I told him at least six times a day for the past week that I felt like I was imposing, he reassured me at least six more times that it was my place as much as his. He didn't want to make it scarier than it is; we are two people living in the same house, who find pleasure in each other's existence. And while it's completely true, he doesn't let me contribute to any of the bills. I get it, he doesn't want me to feel like I'm trapped again, but trapped isn't even a word in the same vicinity as Johnny.

That man makes me feel the least claustrophobic I've ever been. He sleeps with his arm draped over me every night, yet, I can get out of bed whenever I want without feeling like it'll cause an issue. I can ask him to be dominant with me, and I still feel like I can say no if it gets too much, and he'll comply and comfort me until I feel safe again.

I've been having a hard time understanding my feelings towards Johnny, and I know he's been afraid to broach the subject too. It's not that I don't know how I feel about him, because I do, but it's speaking the words out loud to him. I can sit and stew in my own internalized monologue and put it to the back of my mind like it's not important, but as soon as someone else hears what my mind is saying, it becomes a subject that needs to be approached, and I don't like the responsibility that comes with that.

He doesn't want to bring up the subject of *us* because he doesn't want to scare me away. I get that; I'm a wife to another man who has ruined the thought of commitment for me. It still makes me nauseous when I think about it too much and how falling for another man is pushing me into another abusive cycle. But if the therapist podcasts I listen to have taught me anything, it's that there is not one person who is the same as another. One person's 'acting out' is another person's 'sit down and work through'. Past experiences can impact growth or damage. Each chapter in a person's life can determine how they act. Bad experiences don't result in people turning abusive. Good experiences don't result in people being innocent.

Just because Stanley was a toxic man with a respectable job and a lot of power, doesn't mean Johnny will be.

The second I can afford therapy is the second I'll be attending. I've found something with positive potential within Johnny. I'm not allowing my past damage to ruin it, but I also want myself to be prepared for any emotions and reactions I'll need to deal with. I want me to be me again, and that's trusting my heart to do the right thing, even if it hurts.

Looping Poe's lead around the letterbox, I give him a stroke before strolling up to the front door of mine and Stanley's home. Judging from Johnny's note he left me, he'll be arresting this town's corrupt assholes shortly. If Stanley isn't being arrested, he should be at work for another two hours, so I'm free to sneak inside our home, collect my study supplies and any clothes I can fit into my only suitcase before Stanley returns. His car isn't in the driveway and the newspaper sits on the doormat, a clear sign that no one is home. It's a quick in and out before I'm racing to freedom.

I don't want to see him. No. I *can't* see him. I don't trust myself to stay strong if I come face to face with the monster who ruined my life.

Johnny reassured me that Stanley won't be around for much longer and I'll be free soon. I can't ignore the bubbling excitement inside of me at the thought of Stanley rotting in a jail cell.

My hand grasps the cool brass door handle and I push down slightly, waiting for the click. It's unlocked, but that's not unusual. Stanley never locked the door, and I never saw the need to, considering the person who scared me the most, was always inside the house with me.

The scent of out of date food hits me in the face. It's putrid and nauseating, enough for a gag to force my stomach to clench. My eyes are pulled to the kitchen; plates piled along the countertop with moldy food occupying them, the sink is full with cloudy, cold water, and the bin is overflowing with flies buzzing around it, hopping from one soggy food item to another.

Stanley is living in his own hell without a puppet he can force to do the dirty work. Hopefully now he realizes how much work I actually did, every single day, just to make him happy.

My feet are on autopilot as I make my way down the hallway and up the stairs, each step further into this horrid house. But I'm okay. I'm safe because Stanley isn't here.

My eyes glance into our bedroom, and I see the bed is unmade, with Stanley's dirty clothes scattered around the floor. The smell is enough to make my stop in here a quick one, as I dash over to my bedside table, grab all of its contents and leave out the door, shutting it behind me.

I head into my dressing room and place all the things I'm taking with me into a pile, adding all my clothes from my clothing rails, my makeup, underwear, anything I can get my hands on. I don't want to leave a single piece of me behind. Once I'm out of here, I'm never returning, not even to collect things I've left behind.

My full reach can barely touch the suitcase on top of the wardrobe, so I pull my dressing table bench over for a boost. My hands dart out to find balance as I rise to my full height, the bench legs wobbling slightly as I continue to reach higher. Once I can reach the suitcase, I grab the handle and maneuver it around so I can balance its weight between my hands evenly. Even an empty suitcase is heavy. I place it onto the floor and hop off the bench before stuffing everything and anything I own inside.

I don't care about anything that I shared with Stanley. In fact, I don't care about anything in this house, other than the things I owned before I met Stanley. Anything else has connections to him; I don't need any of those. I'm officially cutting ties with my heinous husband and I'm not letting him scare me into staying anymore.

I'm done.

Because this time, I have someone *good* in my corner. Someone who actually cares about me and my own feelings. Not me because I'm young and appealing to a dirty old man.

I scan the almost full case and realize I'm missing one thing. My study materials. I left them downstairs last week before Stanley came home. I can grab them on my way out. Other than that, I'm fully packed and ready to leave this horror movie behind.

Grunting and twisting awkwardly to get me and the suit-case down the stairs, I have to take multiple breaks, the effort causing sweat to gather on my forehead. Each lift is enough to hurt my muscles, although I'm not sure if the muscle aches are from last night with Johnny.

My stomach flutters at the thought of him. All caring and passionate, but dominant in the best way when it comes to pleasing me. A man who puts my needs before his own, I didn't think that was possible.

I want to be back in his arms, his hands in my hair and his skin against mine, creating a union between two people whose souls were destined for each other.

Suitcase wheels slide along the white marble as I bring my suitcase along with me to the living room, ready to collect my study materials and shove them inside before leaving. We are beginning a new journey in life, with the intent to leave this one behind with Stanley, firmly in the past where it belongs.

"We're leaving town. The police are after us." The voice is full of grit and irritation, like one command is enough for a whole city to comply.

Like a shock to the system, my body is frozen on the spot, bile instantly forcing its way up the throat. My calming tactics from the podcast are instantly put into play, but they don't work as true panic claws at my throat. I try deep breathing, but instead, they're fast and chaotic. My brain has decided this is a life or death situation, and I need to get the fuck out of here before my being is terminated.

His car wasn't in the driveway. He never misses work. He shouldn't be here right now.

I scoff lowly at the realization. Maybe this is my destiny afterall. To be a wife to a man whose fist is the only communication he knows. To feel life fade from my body as each day tests my will to live. For death to become more appealing than life itself.

Maybe Johnny was just a taster of what I should've had in life, but instead, it's ripped from me as punishment for my bad decisions.

My eyes fall on Stanley, who's dressed in a dirty shirt, half buttoned, creased slacks and trainers. He has a five o'clock shadow and his eyes are overtaken by dark circles. The TV isn't on, there's no book open in front of him. He just sat glaring at the floor, a hundred yard stare occupying his face.

My study books are inside the coffee table in front of him, but I'm paralyzed with fear. I can't force my legs to move and grab them, even though my freedom is so close, I can taste it. "Sh-shouldn't you be at work?" Razor blades slide my throat as I force the words out, my eyes fast blinking to remove the pending tears. I hide my suitcase in the doorway, praying Stanley doesn't turn and spot it.

"I should be, but I'm not. The disagreement with my wife has affected me more than I thought." His gaze finally turns to me, and the vacant stare looking back at me fills me with dread. "Why did you leave, Elle?"

"I-" I can't get my words out. But I need to. "I thought you were going to kill me." I whisper, the fear from that day washing over me again.

"I should've." He laughs humorlessly. "You disobeyed me, Elle. You know you're to be punished when you disobey your husband." He turns his body back to its original position as his eyes find the blank spot on the carpet. "It doesn't matter anymore. We're leaving town. The police arrested everyone and I'm next."

My eyebrows drop lightly as I try to understand what Stanley is talking about. I never questioned his work when he was at the office for late nights and early mornings. I didn't care what he was doing, as long as he was away from me. But whatever it was, it caught up to him, and he wants me to leave with him.

"What do you mean?" I try to delay, although I'm not sure why. No one is coming to save me.

"The drugs." He scoffs, his hand brushing over his face as his shoulders rise with tension.

Drugs. I gulp. So it is true. I didn't doubt Johnny, but it's hard to believe this small town has a hefty drug operation running. I kind of accepted it was women keeping him occupied.

I don't care if I don't make it out of this alive. I'm not leaving town with him. I'm not allowing him to get what he wants again and again. I'm taking a stand for myself; he will not win this time.

"We can't just leave." My saliva is a wad of cotton in my throat, my eyes burning with tears as fear is the only feeling inside that is charging me.

I barely have time to process Stanley's movement. He's up on his feet and charging at me, my back against the wall. "We can do whatever the fuck I say, darling wife." His yellowed, unbrushed teeth bared as his words hiss in my direction, his eyes are full of rage.

My thoughts are jumbled and I haven't thought of an escape plan yet, so I just say the first thing on my mind. "But what about church?" I question, my eyes unable to hold eye contact for longer than two seconds.

"Church?" He laughs, although he doesn't smile. "There is no church anymore, Elle. Don't you fucking listen? Everyone important has been arrested. This town will collapse without them. That's why we need to run."

I try to make sense of what he's telling me, but without all the information, it feels pointless. I never trusted the men of Charlestown, but to believe they're a part of a drug cartel? My head hurts trying to make sense of it all.

"But-" I don't get to finish my sentence, because Stanley's finger is against my lips, his eyes shooting daggers at me.

His nose trails along my neck, his skin dangerously close to mine. He inhales, before moving his nose to my hand that he forces in front of his face. Another inhale, before dropping my hand.

His expression changes in a second, going from irritated to murderous. "Who is he, Elle?" His tone is deathly calm, but Stanley is anything but. I can see the tension in his jaw as he clenches, and his tensed fist beside my head.

The warning signs are right in front of me, but I'm frozen. I have about two minutes before he loses his shit and I'm a punching bag. I need out. "Who?" I question as neutrally as I can, trying not to anger him any further.

"Don't play fucking dumb. You smell like another man." Another humorless laugh, but this time, his face changes to red. "You're cheating on me, huh? Getting fucked like the slut you are, while your husband is at home, looking after the house you share."

Tears brim my lashes, but I can't find my words. I guess he's not wrong, I am technically married, but it's not like Stanley is with me out of love. I'm being used by him, and he's trying to make me feel guilty for it.

"Who is he, Elle? Tell me what man has been inside this tight pussy." His hand cups my crotch, his grip strong and aggressive. I try to push him off of me, but he doesn't budge. He's rooted to the ground and isn't moving for anyone other than himself.

"Stanley, please-" Wriggling and panicking, my body is acting on fear as I try to get out of the corner I'm backed into.

"Please? Oh, Elle. You should've told me how hungry you were to have cock inside of you, baby. Turn around, I'll fuck you until you're crying for me to stop." His hands are clenched onto my upper arms like he's got super grip and I can't move an inch. My thighs clamp together as a final way of protest and he turns my body so I'm facing the wall, his front against my back. Tears are warming my cheeks as I lose the will to fight, his terrorizing figure making mine look pathetically small. I can't get out of this. I simply have to endure.

"Do you cry when he fucks you? Or are you being the attention seeking whore you are when you decide to be a pathetic wife? I'm the only man who has this!" Stanley roars as venom laces his tone, his hand cupping my breast as his other holds me against the wall. "Your only purpose is to do as I fucking say! I want my dick sucked? You get on your fucking knees. I want to fuck someone who isn't my wife? You turn a blind fucking eye and love me anyway. I want to fuck you up a little and remind you who's in charge? You cry like a fucking baby, but you take it." His voice is a scream in my ear, each word is said with so much conviction that spit attacks my face. "I own you!" His fist is pulled from my breast in a ball, and I clench my eyes, preparing for impact.

But it never comes.

Instead, a delicate click sounds behind Stanley's head. "Take your hands off of her or I will drop you so fucking fast."

I can't even comprehend the relief that fills my body up and gives it another fighting chance. My head turns to the side, and the tattooed sleeve is all I need to see to know it's Johnny. With a gun to Stanley's head, his finger hovers above the trigger a little too calmly. "I'm not going to ask again, Stanley. Let go of her or you'll have more lead than brain tissue in your thick skull." Johnny's eyes are glued to Stanley, his expression dangerously intimidating.

Stanley laughs, but I can hear the wobble in his voice that tells me he's scared. He's never been the man at the bottom of the food chain before. He doesn't know what it's like to comply out of fear of your own life. Stanley releases his grip on my body with a jolt, and I can't stop the whimper from escaping my lips. My back is glued to the wall, hoping it swallows me whole.

Stanley turns painfully slowly to face Johnny, but he drops his raised hands to his side. The sound of the bullet leaving the chamber pierces my ear, and Stanley lets out a wail as blood gushes from his right thigh. A loud thud vibrates through the floor as Stanley collapses, his hands pathetically attempting to stop the bleeding.

"What was that for, man?" Stanley attempts to grip the couch to pull himself up, but he just leaves crimson along the cream fabric, tainting it with more than his bodily fluids.

"For laying a finger on Elle." Johnny's words are terrifyingly calm, but his jaw clenched and his squared shoulders tell me his calmness is just a facade. I can see the vein twitching above his eye as his breathing is heavy and even. A bulletproof police vest frames his tense arm muscles, and I know I shouldn't be looking in this terrifying moment, but I can barely keep my eyes off of him.

Stanley manages to get to his feet, but his hip is lowered on his right side, like he can't put weight on it from the bullet in his leg. Go figure. "I should've known. She's a goddamn slut!" Stanley's finger is pointed in my direction, and I don't miss the look of disgust on his face.

But it doesn't last long, because he's attempting to stride towards Johnny with his fists up and teeth barred. Another pop screeches in my ears as a second bullet is released and deposited straight into Stanley's stomach. "Say one more bad word about her and you'll be six feet under." Johnny growls. Red seeps through Stanley's shirt, the liquid growing by the second. "Doesn't feel great, does it?" Johnny ridicules Stanley as he looks down at him from his full height, his gaze pinned on my abuser like he'll dart towards me any second. "Fearing for your life when you're defenseless. It's sick that you'd get a kick out of this."

"Like you are now?" Stanley can barely form a sentence without heaving for more oxygen, but I don't feel an ounce of worry for him.

Crouching down to Stanley, Johnny waves his gun around. "Exactly like I am now." Johnny nods a sinister smile. "But the difference between me and you, Stanley, is I'll do anything to protect her. That includes putting a bullet into the head of her twisted husband."

Butterflies assault my stomach, but I ignore them. I can't possibly *enjoy* this.

It's a trauma response. It has to be.

"All of this for her?" Stanley barely holds his weight in a sitting position, but he doesn't miss the opportunity to throw poisonous side glances my way, like I'm dirt on the bottom of his shoe. "She's not worth it, Johnny." His voice is a wheeze, his body attempting to tell him to stop insulting me and focus on getting some medical help. "She's a used and abused piece of pussy. Used by me. Abused by me-"

A final bang penetrating the air, my ears throbbing and my sight in disbelief.

A single bullet hole in Stanley's forehead, his eyes opened wide, yet there's no life inside of them. His breathing comes to a halt, his body losing all movement as he just lays there.

I can't peel my eyes away from the dead body laying in front of me, lifeless, yet equally as terrifying as Stanley was when he was alive. My body numb, I can only hear the ringing from the gun and the thrum of my heartbeat as it thumps in my ears. The scent of blood contaminates my nose, and I suddenly feel overwhelmed.

Like he can sense when my body is at its breaking point, Johnny pulls me into his chest, one hand in my hair and the other across my back. He rubs and reassures my worries, placing soft kisses against my forehead. I can't hear what he's telling me as his words are distant and echoing, but I can't focus on anything right now. But I know he's there.

The only thing my eyes want to watch is all of the life draining from my husband's body, like it's a reward for all the pain he forced me to endure.

17

Johnny

I'm a prick for allowing Elle to witness the death of her husband, but my own anger got the better of me. Every bruise, every mark, every tear he caused Elle contaminated my mind and acted as a devil on my shoulder, enticing me to end him.

The second I saw Poe outside, I knew she was inside with Stanley. He had nothing to lose, so if he was going to do anything dangerous, it would've been now. His drug operation was ruined, his friends arrested, his current life ruined. I couldn't allow him to take Elle away with him. Away from me.

If there's one thing I could bless her with, it's ending her abuser. She doesn't have to fear his hands any longer. He's gone and she's finally safe.

Forcing her to stand in that room with her husband's rotting corpse is torture, so I ushered her out as soon as I could pry her eyes off of him. A quick text to my boss informing him Stanley is dead and his body is rotting in his living room was enough information, and shortly after the text was sent, I placed Elle and Poe in my car and drove them to my apartment.

She's in shock. Her life has been a constant pattern for the past three years, and me showing up in Charlestown has changed that. I'm the divide that has caused her life to change, and I just hope she doesn't hate me for it.

A single word hasn't left Elle's lips, but I don't push her. Instead, I carry her from the couch to the bathroom, a hot bath already drawn for her, and I place a kiss on her forehead. I turn to leave to give her privacy, but her small hand grips my arm, stopping me in my tracks. "Stay." Her hushed voice is gentle, her pleading eyes enough for me to stay with her.

My hands find her blood stained clothes and I begin undressing her, the action intimate but not sexual. Her clothes a puddle on the floor, she steps into the bath one foot after the other, submerging her body. Goosebumps attack every inch of her skin, the warm temperature forcing her body to adjust.

I crouch down next to her while staying silent. I want to give her time to accept the traumatic experience she's just gone through, while being a confidant. I don't push her to talk, I'm simply here for her in silence, holding her hand in an attempt to take away some of the pain she's experiencing.

Elle stares aimlessly at her toes that are poking out the water, the lilac nail varnish a splash of color in my neutral bathroom. It doesn't take a therapist to acknowledge her thoughts are eating her up. I can see her mind working behind her ocean eyes, probably finding a way to blame Stanley's own actions on herself.

I admit, I let my feelings get the better of me today. I shouldn't have let my gun release all my pent up anger, but I saw the fear eating Elle up every single day that man was alive. Simply removing him from this world was the only way I could see possible to remove her constant state of anxiety. Sure, it'll take her a hell of a lot of time to emotionally heal, but I'll be by her side throughout it all, if she'll have me. There's not a single step she needs to take where I won't be lifting her upwards.

Specs of crimson scatter along her blonde locks like snowflakes, and while she can't see them, I know it's Stanley gripping onto her one last time. He doesn't get to control her anymore, especially not from the afterlife.

My hand reaches for the shampoo I bought for Elle, and I squeeze a dollop into my hand. The strawberry scent instantly invades my nostrils, and I lather it between my palms. I begin working it into her wet scalp, bubbles forming with each rub. Blood begins dissipating, the remnants of Stanley that once was is no more.

"Is this okay?" I question, beginning to bring the bubbles down towards the ends of her hair. She releases a light hum as she nods, so I carry on washing and massaging. Her usual blonde hair is now a cloud of bubbles, so I scoop water into my hands and rinse off the shampoo. It takes at least five minutes, but I don't see it as a chore. I'm privileged she's letting me do this to her.

I let her wash herself while I get a fresh towel ready, making sure to prepare her pajamas and slippers for when she's finished. The soft cotton towel feels like a warm hug as I open it, ready for Elle to get out of the bath. She hops out without her usual positive step I've been seeing around the apartment, her arms raised as I wrap her up. Grasping her hand, I guide her towards our room and dry her body, before getting her dressed.

The same absent gaze is in her eyes, and it pains me to think there's a part of her that believes this is her fault. Her cheeks flushed and her natural beauty something I have never witnessed before; she's pure in the most gorgeous form. "You're so beautiful, Violet." I hum, crouching in front of her.

Her gaze meets mine and I see a twinge of a smile pull at her lips. But it's gone before I can drink it in, and it's replaced with that absent stare I'm beginning to feel familiar with. "Am I a bad person for wanting him dead?" Her words are barely a whisper, and if I wasn't crouched in front of her, I wouldn't have heard them.

"No." I shake my head, her tear filled eyes breaking my heart. "You could never be a bad person, Elle. He treated you horribly." I grasp both her hands, rubbing reassuring circles with the pads of my thumbs. "Stanley got what he deserved. His actions had a price, and unfortunately for him, he had the easy way out. He should've gotten much worse after the way he treated you."

"He had his demons, and I don't want to speak ill of the dead," a small chuckle escapes Elle's lips. "But I truly believe in karma and it caught up on him."

The small lift of Elle's cheeks are enough to pull a smile from me. "It did." I nod. "He never deserved you."

"I'm not the amazing person you make me out to be, Johnny." Her eyes are fixed onto mine, and that breathtaking smile hasn't faded yet, but the emotion swimming in her irises has the power to pull the small amount of joy she's experiencing in a swift second. "I'm broken and damaged. A girl with a fractured heart. People like me trail shattered glass behind us. We can't escape the shitty life we were given."

"Fractures heal, Elle." I place a kiss on her forehead and sit next to her on the bed, my body facing hers. "The past is the past for a reason. We are given chances in life to learn and grow. You weren't given your life with Stanley, you were forced into it. You now have the opportunity to show the world who Elle Darby really is, and the world is going to love you just as much as I do."

Elle's eyes widen a fraction before she rescues them, but her panicked gaze makes me realize the word I just used. "Love?" Her voice wobbles, but somehow that smile is still plastered on her gorgeous face.

"I'm sorry, I-" I scramble to find an explanation, something that won't scare her away from the stupidly casual confession I just made. But I'm not going to avoid my feelings for her. She owns me, every inch of my being. I didn't know my heart could beat for two before I met her. All I knew was one night stands and my job, but she shone this light in front of me, giving me a taste of what living life with my heart could be like. "This isn't how I wanted to tell you and after tonight," I shake my head, scoffing at my sudden loss of words. "You don't have to do anything with it, bury it if you need to, but I need to tell you how I feel before I lose my chance.

"I live my life in black and white and the only thing that keeps me going is my job, but you showed me a world of color, Violet. Existing isn't living, and until I met you, I thought they were the same thing, but you've shown me a side of this world where living is a blessing when you're here. My heart was stone, but I feel each beat whenever you're around, Elle Darby, and I never want to lose you "

Is it too late to backtrack? The tears covering her lash line tells me it's too late, but those words have left the confines of safety inside of me, I can't take them back.

"Johnny," she's breathless and I'm nearly falling off a cliff, fearing I've made her night more traumatic than it already was. "I'm not easy. I thought I had been scared off of relationships from the hell Stanley put me through, but being with you is easy and something I've never experienced. I've never had someone care for Poe as much as I do, and he deserves the world more than anyone I know. I'm not saying I don't feel the same way, because I do." Blushed cheeks bloom and that smile seems to be here to stay, but she's avoiding eye contact like it's the plague. I don't mind though; she needs a safe space to say how she feels. I'm not going anywhere. "I want this," her fingers move between us before her hand falls back into my palm. "I just need a slow pace, so I can learn to love myself again. But I also need you and this normality we've created. "I understand if you don't want to wait for me, but if you do, I'd love to have you by my side for whatever life throws our way."

I can't stop the full blown grin from appearing. We've danced around our feelings for each other for so long, it feels like our bodies knew how we felt about each other before our minds could voice it. "I'm not going anywhere, Violet."

"You know it's a daisy, right?" Elle teases, playfully squinting at me like I don't remember our first conversation.

"Mmhm." I nod. "But violet is my new favorite color, because it's you." I hum.

"You know what my favorite thing is?" Elle croaks, her smile replaced with need pooling in her eyes.

"What?" I respond, my eyes fixed on hers.

"This," she whispers, her hands placed on my cheeks, her lips closing the gap between us as she meets mine.

My cock is awakened the second I taste her sweet mouth. Passionate and sensual, the outside world that surrounds us slowly fades away, and I'm sucked into a world of Elle. My hands find her cheeks as I tilt her head back and my tongue enters her mouth, her mouth widening and allowing access.

Scooping her up into my arms, I carry her up the bed, her legs gripping my waist. The action makes my cock throb, her entrance only covered by a thin piece of fabric. My cock buried in her pussy is one of my favorite places to be, and her lust filled moans are my favorite thing to hear.

I'm almost panting at the sight of her, her breathing erratic and desire swimming in her ocean eyes. I'm about to rip her clothes off and take her perfect tits in my mouth, but her hand gripping my forearm pauses my movements. "Lay on your back." She directs me, soft and gentle, but a direction nonetheless.

I squint, eager to see where this is going. She nods at me, a way to get me moving, and sure enough, I've rolled onto my back, my eyes glued on her for any clues as to where this is going.

She's on her knees looking down at me, until she hops off the bed and stands at the base. She crawls on top of me, and lifts my shirt over my head, I sit up slightly to help her, my bare torso exposed and kissed by the light chill in the air. Her small fingers looped in my jeans next, and she pulls downwards with force. My cock springs free as soon as the waistband is below my crotch, my cock beading with precum. Elle's tongue glides along her bottom lip as she gawks at my cock. Impatience takes over me as I kick off my jeans and grasp Elle, but she wags her finger at me and pushes my chest back down. "Just relax." She murmurs, a mischievous smile growing on her gorgeous face.

"I can't keep my hands off of you, Violet. How am I supposed to relax when you're so fucking perfect?" I'm restless because I just want her in my arms.

"Like this," she purrs. Sitting on her knees between my legs, her hand grips my shaft and her mouth is placed over my cock.

A low rumble escapes my lips, pleasure creating a rainbow behind my eyes as her warm mouth swirls and sucks my tip. "Fuck, Violet." I groan, my hands finding their way into her scalp. She hums against my dick, the vibration a wave of satisfaction.

She begins bobbing her head up and down, her cheeks sucked in as her mouth sits in a perfect 'O' shape, her eyes sultry as they pin me.

I can't take my fucking eyes off her. Not when she runs her tongue from my base to my tip. Not when her hands massage my balls. And especially not when she licks every drop of precum from the head of my cock.

Her gags are fucking intoxicating as my cock hits the back of her throat over and over again, her eyes damp and drunk on pleasure but she doesn't let up, continuing to deep throat my cock like a pro.

Satisfaction builds deep in my gut and takes over every inch of my body like a possession. Every nerve inside of me is bubbling, tempting me to fall over the edge. "You're so fucking perfect, baby. I'm going to come in your sweet mouth." Her moan of approval is enough guidance for me to explode inside of her hot mouth. Thick ropes of come release each time Elle's head bobs up and down, sucking me through my orgasm. I can barely see her though, because my vision is blurry from pure fucking pleasure, my audible groans are fill the air. I fight the urge to fuck her mouth, but my cock tapping the back of her throat is good enough for me. Waves of ecstasy flood through me, my body weightless from the tear inducing orgasm she just put me through.

Elle slow's her pace, and once I've ridden my orgasm, she releases my cock with a pop and swallows my come.

Fuck.

Such a good girl.

"So fucking perfect." I coo, bringing her body on top of mine. I roll on top of her, my mouth crashing against hers, the taste of salt invading my tastebuds.

I pave a path of soft kisses down her chest, but I don't have a chance to get any lower. "I need you inside of me." Elle pants, her hand stroking my already erect cock, her teeth nibbling her bottom lip.

I can't say no to those pleading eyes. "I need to be inside of you." I grunt, my hands yanking her pajamas off so she lays exposed beneath me. Her perfect tits bounce free, her nipples pebbled from the quick exposure to the cool air. I take one into my mouth, flicking and nibbling, while I massage the other between my finger and thumb. She tries to thrust into my cock, but I'm enjoying teasing her. I like the fire that roars in her eyes when she can't get her own way.

She's a picturesque sight, like a goddess sent from heaven herself. Yet her moans are sinful and erotic, the kind of sound that makes my dick hard the second I hear them.

Her exposed pussy is glistening with need, her legs bent and ready for me. "You're dripping for me, baby. Are you desperate for my cock to feel your tight pussy?" I tease her, my cock swiping up and down her folds, collecting her juices.

She whimpers, her legs instinctively falling open as she nods.

My finger dips inside her pussy, instantly pulling a moan from her precious lips. I withdraw, and place my soaked finger in my mouth. My eyes shut as I savour how fucking good she tastes, humming my approval. "So fucking perfect, baby."

Leaning over her, I take her mouth in mine, line my cock up with her entrance, and in once thrust, I'm buried deep inside of her. We gasp in unison, drinking up each other's moans as I rock my hips back and forwards, her slickness coating my cock.

Her pussy clamps around my dick the longer I thrust, her moans becoming more erratic and desperate, like she's needed this all day. After the eventful day she's had, I'm privileged she's letting me fuck the stress out of her. I want her so distracted from today that the only thing she can do is scream while I'm deep inside of her.

I'm buried to the hilt, my thrusts chaotic and out of time, yet the only thing I can focus on is the way Elle's brows pull together when her orgasm is catching up on her. The higher her moan, the closer it is, and in the blink of an eye, her pussy milks my cock as she clenches, her body's automatic response as she comes. Her hands try to grip anything she can hold onto, but she's in a daze of pleasure, unable to focus on anything.

She's gasping like a girl dehydrated, her hair a mess, and her eyes closed, yet she looks fucking magnificent. "You're dripping on my cock, baby. That's a good fucking girl." We both look down in sync at where our bodies meet, and the sight alone is enough to push me over the edge. Soaked and hard, my cock bobs in and out of her entrance, the warmth of our come wrapping a blanket around my cock. "Fuck, Elle." I grunt, my head falling back as white spots contaminate my vision. I can barely grasp onto her hips as my muscles lose their strength, my body lost in waves of euphoria. I want to stay in this world of bliss I'm lost into, deep inside my girl as we come in unison.

My thrusts slow as we come down from our pleasure, my body falling onto the bed next to her. She's barely holding onto consciousness as her eyes flutter closed, her head nuzzling into my shoulder and my arm wrapped around her waist. I scatter soft kisses along her forehead as I listen to her calm breathing, soaking in the stillness around us.

We were fucking made for each other. Two people coming together as one. A partnership that can never be beaten.

I never want to face life without my girl by my side.

18

ELLE

I f it were up to me, Stanley would be left in the dust and handed over to the state to deal with, but someone thought he should have a final resting place with a ceremony. I don't know who organized his funeral and I don't know who paid for it. All I know is I didn't get a single say and that's something I'm ecstatic about. My guess is Mayor Clyde's wife is responsible, who probably received instruction from her husband while he sits behind bars. Or Sheriff Beasley, considering he's his brother.

Because of the severity of their crimes, they aren't permitted to attend the funeral at the same time as everyone else. They are all given allocated slots to say their final goodbyes so they don't cross paths. Not one of the wives of the arrested have kept me in the loop. I assume that's because they heard about me and Johnny, but I'm not sad about it. I'm happy to build a big wall in between before and after and move on with my life.

It doesn't look great that I'm not attending the funeral service as his mourning wife, but I couldn't put myself through the torture. I can't sit and listen to Charlestown residents sing Stanley's praises, saying what a loss we've all experienced and that he's such a great person. They never knew the real Stanley. They saw the focused councilor and the passionate church goer. Not the temper ridden husband who solved his problems through gaslighting and the power of his fist. That was the real Stanley, not the mask he wore when facing the public.

I never realized how poisonous he really was until I tasted a stable relationship. I knew he was bad, my constant state of anxiety told me that, but I haven't felt a twinge of anxiety since being with Johnny. Sure, my guard sometimes reminds me I can never fully trust anyone, but the way he treats me like I paved the earth for us to walk on is throwing a sledge hammer at my guard. He hasn't once raised his voice or given me ultimatums. I have a choice in everything we do. He treats Poe like he's his own dog, even letting him sleep in the bed with us. I can actually study without fearing I'll be in trouble. This is what a mutual bond should be like, and I'm thankful I took the step and explored this life with Johnny.

He's the best thing that has ever happened to me. After Poe, of course.

"Are you sure you want to do this?" Johnny's arms wrap around mine as his warmth creates a safe barrier around me.

I nod, looking over my black dress in the mirror. "Watching him being lowered into the ground is my final 'fuck you' to him. I want him to know I got the last laugh."

"That you did, baby." He places a sweet kiss on my forehead before adjusting his tie. He looks so dapper in a suit, I'm debating whether to attend the funeral at all, just so I can spend my time entwined with Johnny instead.

I gaze at my hair, studying the length before I clip half up. It's grown since Stanley died. It's actually long enough to plait now, which Johnny loves doing. Any chance he gets to play with my hair, he's there in record time. I didn't think I could ever let anyone lay a finger on it with the impending fear it's going to be yanked, but I took myself by surprise when a single thought didn't even cross my mind. Instead, I actually felt relaxed. Like all my worries are released when Johnny's fingertips are massaging my scalp.

"We better get going." Johnny glances at his watch before finding his car keys and checking Poe has enough water and food to last him while we're out. He won't admit it, but he loves the role of dog dad. Sometimes I catch him having a full conversation with Poe, and while Poe can't reply, that doesn't stop Johnny from talking to our boy.

Glancing at my flats, I make sure I'm wearing appropriate footwear before giving Poe a kiss goodbye and heading out the door, Johnny following closely behind me. He opens the car door for me and lets me hop in before closing it, and we make a swift getaway towards the graveyard.

It wasn't hard to find out the details for the funeral; Stanley had a whole dedication page in the newspaper for him. He's only been dead a week and he's already getting all the exposure he'd want. But it won't last long. He'll soon be forgotten about and the name Stanley Adams will be as forgettable as he deserves to be. Memorializing a man who abused his power isn't a way to remember his supposed bravery. It's a travesty.

Charlestown church is crawling with people; town occupants and the press, all here to pay their respects and mourn the life lost. I wonder if they'd still mourn him if he hurt them the way he hurt me. Maybe they'd be watching from a distance in the treeline, like me and Johnny are.

Johnny respected my wishes to attend from a distance. His concerns were how I'd feel, but I reassured him I want to see him one last time, beneath me. His power can't control me anymore when he's helpless and dead.

A large wooden coffin is carried from the church by men dressed in black, while members of Charlestown follow closely behind, sobbing and drying their tears with tissues. The church bells toll loudly for Stanley's final descent, a symbol of a loss of life.

Loss isn't the word I'd use, but he did, in fact, lose in the end.

I watch as wives cuddle into each other, offering comfort where their husbands can't. I wonder if they find it hard to accept that their husbands won't ever have the opportunity to console them again, considering they're in jail. Are they mourning Stanley or the loss of their husbands?

I don't know how much they knew, but to stand by a man who abused the system and used their power as a right of passage puts them as low as their husbands. It's never too late to do the right thing, and life doesn't end when a marriage breaks down. It's an opportunity to create a new path for yourself and give yourself the life you deserve.

The priest begins a speech, but I can't keep my brain focused on him long enough to understand what he's saying. Instead, my eyes are glued on the oak coffin, every inch of hatred inside of me is aimed towards the dead man. I can't find it in me to feel guilty for him. He paved his own path in life, he can't be angry that his sins finally caught up on him.

Embarrassment fills me at the sight of weeping attendees, their crocodile tears as convincing as their sobs. If I hadn't known any better, I'd say they are actually in mourning. But I do know better, and I know they're only crying because of the hell their husbands have recently put them through. It's humiliating to explain your husband is in prison for a drug trade gone wrong. I'm glad I don't have to join them on that one.

Johnny stands behind me in silence, his arms wrapped around my waist as my back meets his front. His chin rests on my head, and I count his slow breaths. Each one even and balanced, like he's at peace watching my dead husband find his destiny. He doesn't usher me on or encourage me to leave. He simply stands with me, for hours, as we watch Stanley's body lower into the ground and attendees throw petals onto him, before the undertaker piles mud on top of him.

Stanley's gone and he can never hurt me again.

Emotion overcomes me, my eyes brimming with tears and my chest heaving rapidly. I don't feel sad. I don't know what

I feel, but relief is the feeling planted in my gut that drives my tears to release themselves. I never thought I'd be free of that man, but my knight in shining armor appeared like a wish I'd never thought would come true.

"Hey," Johnny turns to face me, concern lacing his voice. "It's okay, baby. He's gone. He can never hurt you again." Wrapping me into his chest, safety and solace form a blanket around me. "Wanna go spit on his grave?"

I can't stop the laugh bubbling in my chest. With damp eyes and lifted cheeks, I nod.

The graveyard is empty and the sky is a hue of gray as the night settles around us. I don't know how long we've been here; long enough for my feet to ache and my stomach to grumble. Slow steps towards Stanley's fresh grave create an empty pit in my stomach. Something inside of me tells me I should be upset; my husband is dead. But he wasn't really my husband. He was a temporary way through life. That's the thing with temporaries, they aren't here to last. And I thank my lucky stars that mine came to an end.

I glance at the stone sign, Stanley's name carved into it as a permanent place holder. That's my last laugh, he can't leave here, but I can. The stupid bastard didn't even bother with a will, so every penny of his fortune, our home included, falls onto me. The house is going up for sale and me and Johnny are comfortable for the foreseeable future with Stanley's bank account.

I guess I got the last laugh, Stanley.

"Hey, Violet." Johnny's hand grips my cheek, a sensual kiss placed on my lips. All traces of negativity evaporate from my body the second I'm sucked into a world of Johnny. "Want to give him one last fuck you?" I can see the mischief lining his smirk, and my stomach flutters at the sight of him.

I nod, curious as to what he's implying.

"Lay down." His direction is soft but leading, his grip on my cheek sending heat straight to my core. I know what this is leading to, and there's only one place I want to lay while experiencing this.

A final fuck you to you, Stanley.

I lay directly on top of Stanley's fresh grave, empowerment and control filling my body. Johnny follows me, his body over mine, encompassing me with his muscular build. His lips find mine, soft and sweet, but each second he's on me, passion erupts a fire inside of us, like I'm gasoline and he's a match. His erect cock teases my entrance, but he doesn't unbutton himself, instead, he grips my tights and panties, and yanks them down in one swift pull. My pussy exposed, I feel the cool air on my skin, a thrilling reminder we are out in the open.

Wet kisses fall down my neck, towards my stomach, Johnny's eyes never leaving mine. Desire fills his eyes and his tongue wets his lips. Like a man starved, his eyes fall on my core, a growl escaping his lips. "So fucking wet for me, Violet. This pussy is mine and mine only." I can't stop the whine from escaping my lips.

My legs are pushed upwards, my pussy on full display, wet and ready for him. "Fuck." He hums, but I don't have time to relish in his mesmerized state, because his mouth is against my pussy, drinking every inch of me in. He eats and sucks, paying special attention to my clit. Soft nibbles and flicks send jolts to my core, my body finding that familiar pleasure.

My hands are in his hair as I grind against his mouth, his hums of approval vibrating against my clit. He licks from my entrance to my clit, there's not an inch of me that he leaves untouched. I feel like a goddess whenever Johnny pleasures me, his eyes never straying from my body.

"I want your come dripping down my chin, Violet. I want to taste you every single second of every day." I can barely hear his words as my ears thrum with satisfaction. Whimpers and moans escape my lips from the absolute bliss Johnny is creating between my legs. I'll never get sick of this.

My body can barely hold onto reality, I'm so close to falling over the edge, but Johnny inserts a finger, followed by another, and finger fucks me. I'm overwhelmed and the desire constantly forming in between my legs is causing my vision to blur. I can't focus, every single worry inside of me is replaced by the magic Johnny is creating.

"Johnny!" I moan, my release forming so thick I can't hold on.

"Come for me, baby." His instruction is enough for me to let go. Stars blind my vision and ecstasy fills my veins as my body releases my orgasm. I'm weightless, the only form of stability is my hands in Johnny's hair as I fuck his face the longer I come into his mouth. My body shakes violently as I chant his name over and over, my pussy clenching around his fingers while my clit throbs against his tongue.

He slows his pace and eventually comes to a stop, and I groan at the instant loss I feel the second he retracts his fingers. He sits upwards as he watches over me, a delicious smile taking over his face. His chin glistens in the small amount of light that surrounds us, and comfort fills me at the knowledge that he's the only person that can make me come that fucking good.

His fingers that were inside of me find their way into his mouth as he licks my juices clean. He releases a moan of satisfaction, savoring the taste. "That's my fucking girl." He coos, leaning over me and placing a kiss against my lips. He pulls my panties and tights back up and pulls me to my feet, pulling me close to his chest. "Fuck you, Stanley." He grunts, a satisfied smirk on his face.

Fuck you, indeed.

19

Epilogue

ELLE

Six months later

"Miss Darby!" One of my kindergarten children calls my name as he struggles to get his shoes on. Padding over towards him, I crouch down and slide his shoe on, fastening the velcro before patting him on the head.

It was a long six months to get my teaching qualification, but it was the best experience I ever put myself through. I enjoyed the deadlines and the hours I spent with my face in a book. I love learning, especially when it means I can do the one job

I have always dreamt of doing, without the threat of a petty crime glooming over my head.

Ringing of the end of the day bell fills my classroom and the kids are immediately up onto their feet, grabbing their bags and dashing out the door. "Walking feet!" I yell, in hopes they actually listen to me. It's in vain, they're too focused on their chance to find their parents.

I soak in my end of day peace as I sit at my desk, flicking through my weekly plan of activities. The focus for this week is nature and what our outside world looks like when winter approaches. It's an excuse for Christmas films and lots of arts and crafts, therefore, lots of activities to focus on their fine motor skills. Coloring, painting, designing, the kinds of things that get the children fully engrossed and to find their artistic side.

My phone buzzes on my desk, and I grab it to take a peek at the notification.

How are my girls doing? I miss you.

Warmth fills my heart at Johnny's text, he never goes a day without telling me he misses me when I'm not with him. My hand falls on my stomach as I rub our baby girl, her little kicks becoming stronger each day.

Doing good. We miss you. Can't wait to be in your arms.

I thought honeymoon fazes didn't last this long, but we are in a permanent state of adoration for each other that I'll never get sick of it. The only thing that makes me sick is pickles, and that's all thanks to our baby girl.

I'm not sure how it happened, but one morning I woke up with nausea that could make me pass out. Well, I do know how it happened, the logistics itself, but I was on birth control. I took it religiously while with Stanley, because carrying a mini him was a nightmare I could never face. Plus, Stanley refused to believe medical professionals, but he was infertile. He was adamant the three different consultants we saw didn't know what they were talking about, but at his age, his swimmers weren't strong enough.

I'm certain I still took birth control while with Johnny, considering it was part of my daily routine. We were taking things slow and a baby was never in our three year plan, but our girl is a fighter and demanded she's here to stay.

Once I finish filing some paperwork and get the classroom prepared for tomorrow, I pack up my things and begin my daily stroll home. Johnny has tried convincing me to get a car after I sold the one Stanley got me, but I've grown to love the short ten minute stroll through Charlestown, back to our apartment.

Charlestown has gone through a major change within the past six months. With a new mayor, new councilors, and a new police department, the corruption here is a thing of the past. They actually do what their job role entails instead of breaking a few rules for the fun of it.

The community has a lot of new faces, and the old ones seem to have relocated. Those tortured wives with felon husbands have left the town they once loved and didn't leave a forwarding address. I guess they want to keep a low profile wherever they moved to. It's got to be a bitch explaining your husband is locked up because his greed got the better of him.

I decided to take a detour on my route home, to give myself the opportunity to rewrite the past. Places can hold bad memories too, but if people deserve a second chance, why can't buildings?

It's a little chilly in Charlestown today as fall comes to an end, but I love the way the cool air kisses my cheeks, giving them a tinge of pink. I'm wrapped up warm in my lilac peacoat and my gloves, my chest length hair warming my neck and head. The waves crash against one another in the background and the clouds form a perfect autumnal backdrop on Charlestown's seaside.

The anxiety is brewing in my stomach, but I reassure myself that *that* life can't hurt me anymore. Inhaling cool breaths before breathing them out, the heat creates small clouds of mist in the chilly air. With one foot in front of the other, I begin passing my old home, the one where my nightmares came true. Two children play on the front lawn, one swinging on a tire swing they set up to the large tree, and the other pushing them. Compassion blooms in my chest. They look happy.

I am, too.

My feet take the stroll back to our apartment, greeting Charlestown residents as I pass them. My hand finds its way onto my stomach as I rub gently. I didn't see myself having children, but Johnny has shown me a new world. I finally want that life with the picket fence and the perfect small town. When he's next to me, I feel like I can conquer anything thrown my way.

Taking a chance on Johnny was the best choice I ever made.

The smell of garlic chicken wafts down the corridor before I reach our door, instantly forcing a growl from my stomach. I chuckle, my eyes falling on my bump. "I'm hungry too, baby girl. Daddy sure is a good cook."

The click from the handle sounds, and the warmth from the oven heats my body the second I open the door. Johnny lightly hums along to *The Pretender* by the Foo Fighters from the kitchen, the sizzle from the hob filling the air.

I place my bag down and take off my coat and shoes, giving Poe strokes and kisses, before waltzing into the kitchen to watch him. My cheeks lift instantly at the sight of him in a black tee and joggers, a tea towel draped over his shoulder, while frying asparagus. "Anyone ever told you how great you are at cooking?" I speak over the radio as I lean against the wall.

Instantly pausing his cooking, he strolls over to me, one hand around my waist and the other on my cheek, his lips planted against mine. "You tell me every single day." We chuckle in unison. "Missed you, baby. Dinner is ready in five."

I nod, planning to get into something comfier, but Johnny pauses my movements. He crouches down and kisses my stomach, a routine he's been doing since we found out we were pregnant.

He's going to be the best dad and I can't wait to witness it.

My pajamas are already laid out for me on the bed; the sight of Johnny preparing almost everything for me makes my heart bloom. A single day doesn't go by where he's not taking care of me. Our relationship started from him looking out for me, and he's never stopped. Like the purehearted person he is, he always puts me before himself. Even before I was pregnant, my needs came before his own, and anything I needed, it was placed in front of me before I had the chance to get it myself.

Hopping into the silk pajamas, I pull open my bedside drawer to put on some lip balm, but the velvet box catches my eye instead. It's been sitting in here for a month, patiently waiting for its exit. Johnny's proposal wasn't a traditional one. In fact, most people would have taken my reaction to offense, but he understands me. There was no one knee and no question of marriage. Instead, Johnny gifted me the engagement ring with the purpose of marriage, but not until I'm ready. From my past of bad marriages, Johnny knew they left a bad taste in my mouth, and he didn't want me to agree if I wasn't ready. So, I have the ring, and his confession of wanting to marry me. All I have to do is tell him when, if ever, I'm ready to take the next step.

I think the time has finally come.

Johnny

Dishes are perfectly organized around the table ready for me and Elle to sit and eat, with cutlery in their places and fresh pomegranate juice poured into glasses. I fill up Poe's food bowl with chicken and his favorite vegetables and whistle him over, but he doesn't come. "Poe, dinner!" I call, his usual excitement not present.

I frown, unsure on why he isn't coming over. Making the rounds of the apartment, I check all the rooms to find him, but he's not here. A final check in our bedroom to see if he's with Elle, and relief immediately washes over me. He's sitting with his mom, his chin nuzzled into Elle's stomach as he breathes slowly.

Accomplishment blooms in my chest as I take in the sight before me. My family is so goddamn perfect, I couldn't have wished for a better partner and a better dog. I found my purpose within these beings in front of me, and I never want to face a day in life without them by my side.

My eyes are fixed on Elle's, a twinge of mischief swimming in her ocean blue eyes. I squint, unsure of what she's up to, but then her gaze falls to the bedside table, before bouncing back to me. I follow where she's looking, and I see the velvet ring box sitting open, with the violet colored stone glistening in the light, the silver band decorated with small diamonds.

I'm taken aback by her encouragement. I proposed with the understanding that Elle may never say yes, and I was okay with that. I wanted the proposal to mean more than a ring on a finger. It was a promise I made to her, that I'll be her protector and defender in life, and that she's my forever. I needed her to know that, and no matter how long she needs to face her past trauma, I'd be with her every step of the way.

"Seriously?" I question, shock making my voice wobble. She nods, sitting up slightly so she's not slouched. I grasp the ring box and pull out the ring and I crouch on one knee in front of her.

"We don't have to do the traditional proposal." She laughs, her eyes rolling sarcastically.

"You deserve it." I encourage, taking her left hand in mine. "Elle Darby, my violet, the only woman I've ever loved. It would be an absolute honor to have you as my wife, the woman who owns my heart and soul in its entirety, and the mother of our children. I promise to protect you and love you for as long as I live, to support every decision you make, and to respect your wishes in life. You're my violet in a field of leaves, and I want to live in a world of lilac until I die." Her lash line is filled with tears, but her smile is full of happiness. "Will you marry me?" My voice croaks as I hold back tears, the chance to have this woman as my wife is pulling at my heartstrings.

"Yes." She coos, her lips crashing against mine. I slide the ring onto her finger and she jumps up like a child on its birthday, before wrapping her arms and legs around me.

"I love you, Elle Darby."

"I love you too, Johnny Miller." Her lips against mine, perfectly made for each other.

My fiance is the definition of a kind soul. She may have been dealt the shittest hand of cards in life, but I'm forever in awe at how well she handles herself. I don't know what I did to deserve a woman as amazing as her, but now that I have her, I'm never letting her go. My only aim in life is to make happiness her permanent emotion, because watching her bloom into this breathtaking person is like watching an ethereal violet flowering.

It's a journey of life; no matter how many times a violet flowers, they always rebuild themselves when a little light is shone on them. Regrowth is her superpower, and I'll never get sick of watching her bloom.

The End

Acknowledgements

Fiancé, as always, I couldn't do this without you. Never moaning when I'm up late at night writing or agreeing to watch a movie with you, but only half paying attention while I plot a book. Thank you for celebrating my little wins for me, even if it's just relaying feedback from my books. My life would be so dull without you. I love you 3000. My true blue, always.

Ellen, my constant hype girl and a perfect friend. Thank you so so so much for your constant support and always getting excited when I tell you even the smallest of details about my books. I could actually cry at how much love you show me and my books. You keep me going with how much you big me up. I'm forever grateful for you, your messages and your voice notes. They're my favourite!

Ria, my editor, who is always so understanding and is an absolute gem. I count my lucky stars that I found you because I would be so lost without ya!

My BETA and ARC readers, thank you for even showing interest in my book and wanting to read it! It may be as simple as reading another book to you, but to me, it's such a big achievement. I still can't believe people want to read my silly little words on paper!

Liv, for making me feel important when asking me author advice and questions and for always supporting me. I love that you trust me to give you guidance and I am always here for you whenever you need me. Hearing about your future plans to write makes me so happy. Also your voice notes are my favourite.

Also, a shout out to my siblings and my friends for your support and encouragement. To my bestie who doesn't read darker romance yet picked up my book for the kindle page reads. Ilysm.

To anyone who is reading my book or book/s – thank you from the bottom of my heart. Whether you enjoyed it or not, thank you for taking the time to read. You'll never know how much you mean to this baby author.

About the Author

Esme Lennon is an indie author from England. Her love for reading first started on Wattpad, where she read a few too many Marvel fanfics, and also began her writing journey. This led Esme onto booktok, immersing her in a world of contemporary romance and dark romance books. This gave her the courage and inspiration to write her own books and explore her own fictional worlds.

In her free time, Esme loves to lose herself in a good book and spend time with her fiancé, friends, family, and her pup. She's a complete home bird; you'll find Esme snuggled up on the sofa, re-watching Marvel movies with her better half.

Also by Esme

Fancy reading about a stalker and his little snowflake? Read Little Snowflake now! Available on Amazon and Kindle Unlimited.

How about a marriage of convenience romance story with a grumpy billionaire and a girl who's determined to save her family? Read Power Play now! Available on Amazon and Kindle Unlimited.